"Maybe you have to know the darkness before you can appreciate the light."
– Madeline L'Engle

I0716759

SYSTEMA PARADOXA

ACCOUNTS OF CRYPTOZOOLOGICAL IMPORT

VOLUME 24

BLIND DEVOTION

A TALE OF THE VAN METER VISITOR

AS ACCOUNTED BY TY DRAGO

NEOPARADOXA

Pennsville, NJ

2025

PUBLISHED BY
NeoParadoxa
A division of eSpec Books
PO Box 242
Pennsville, NJ 08070
www.especbooks.com

Copyright © 2025 Ty Drago

ISBN: 978-1-956463-77-4
ISBN (ebook): 978-1-956463-76-7

All rights reserved. No part of the contents of this book may be reproduced or transmitted in any form or by any means without the written permission of the publisher.

All persons, places, and events in this book are fictitious and any resemblance to actual persons, places, or events is purely coincidental.

Interior Design: Danielle McPhail
www.sidhenadaire.com

Cover Art: JW Harp
Cover Design: Mike and Danielle McPhail, McP Digital Graphics
Interior Illustration: JW Harp

Copyediting: Greg Schauer and John L. French

Dedication

For Alex, with love.
Welcome to the family!

*For five days in the Fall of 1903, a series of bizarre encounters
haunted the small town of Van Meter, Iowa. These unprecedented
and repeated sightings of a unique and heretofore unknown "
cryptid" terrorized the community and should, once all was
revealed, have drawn national or even global attention.
By all rights, these events should have changed the world.*

This is the story of why they didn't.

Based on real events.

Chapter One

September 29, 1903

"Hank, get up!"

I was dreaming my favorite dream, the one about kissing a girl. No, scratch that. Kissing *the* girl. Her long blonde hair smelled of strawberries and she was beautiful. Not made-up beautiful like some of the church ladies who dropped money in my hat and told themselves it made them "good." No, my girl was beautiful in the way nature made her, with skin like cream, smooth and perfect.

My dream girl — the girl of my dreams.

"Hank, wake up! I need your help!"

I opened my eyes, the dream vanishing like the nonsense it was.

But the dream girl remained. In fact, it was my sweet sixteen herself who stood over me, poking me with her cane.

"Hank! Dang it, Hank!"

"Alex?" I asked blearily. The bed of straw I'd made for myself rustled as I sat up. "Al? That you?"

"Of course, it's me! I'm standing right in front of you!"

"It's pitch dark in here."

She paused and replied in a gentler tone, "Oh. I didn't think…"

I fumbled for the old lantern and lit it with one of only four matches left in my little carboard box. Its glow filled the abandoned shed that I'd made my home for the past few months. The shed and its land used to belong to old Mary Durbin, who died without family last spring, leaving the property to the town. It'd be years before anyone decided what to do with it, which suited me fine. I enjoyed having a steady roof over my head.

You see, I was the town beggar and son of the local drunkard. Ever read *Huckleberry Finn*? Well, in Van Meter, Iowa that was me, and it was buckets less "romantic" than Twain made it out to be. Trust me on that.

Finally fully awake, I looked up—*gazed*, really—at Alexandra Harrer.

She was a slip of a girl, slender as a reed and barely half my height. Okay, that was exaggeration, but Alex had taught me that writers exaggerate the way politicians lie, so I supposed it was all right.

Yeah, I was a writer, or wanted to be, or *would* be, if Alex had anything to say about it.

We'd known each other since she'd come to town eight months ago, moving in with her spinster aunt after her folks died. I still didn't know much about what happened. But I knew she missed them. Alex Harrer walked in loneliness like it was her favorite pair of shoes.

"Come on!" she insisted, taking my hand with that weird accuracy she sometimes showed.

"What time is it?" I asked, climbing stiffly to my feet.

"Past midnight," she replied, as though it were the most normal thing in the world. "Hurry up!"

"What's going on?" But, instead of answering, she pulled me toward the open shed door, her cane tapping the floor with every step.

Did I fail to mention that Alexandra Harrer was blind?

Unseeing from birth, she navigated this world at the end of a hickory cane, a gift from her wealthy, spinster aunt.

Alex was also a good friend to me, the only one I really had. True, she didn't look at me, so to speak, the way I looked at her. But I couldn't blame her for that. I was nobody's "dream boy." At seventeen, I was tall and scrawny and rarely bathed, with a rat's nest of hair that reached to my shoulders. I hadn't set foot in a schoolhouse in six years and what reading and writing I knew came entirely from Alex and her patient lessons.

Her greatest gift to me, other than kissing dreams, had been what she dubbed my bibliomania—a big word that simply meant I liked books.

And someday I meant to write one.

Alex pulled me through the shed door and out into the night. It was warm for late September, with the clear sky awash in stars. Ahead stretched an open field that ended at Grand Street, just a few blocks from Main.

"Slow down, will you?" I exclaimed as she dragged me through the tall grass, heedless of gopher holes.

But she ignored me, her cane testing the ground as she charged along, moving fast enough that I had to jog to keep pace.

Then upon reaching Grand, Alex suddenly paused and stood statue still.

"What—" I began.

"Shhh!"

I shushed.

"This way!" she declared, hurrying up the street toward Main. "I think she's close!"

"Who's close?"

"Shhh!"

Irritably, I demanded, "Why am I here if I ain't supposed to say nothing?"

"Try that again," she said without breaking stride.

"Try what again?"

"Poor English."

I groaned. "You ain't my teacher right now, Al. What's going on?"

Again, her manner became softer, more like the Alex Harrier I'd come to know. "I'm sorry, Hank. I know I must seem crazy. But something's happened... *is happening,* something I never thought would."

"What's happening? Dang it all, Alex. Wait a second and talk to me!"

"I can't!" And, for the first time, I noticed tears in her eyes. "If anybody sees her..."

I almost asked, "Sees who?" But then a sound hit my ears, distant but approaching fast, moving along Main Street from the west.

Alex turned her sightless eyes toward the rumbling noise. "What *is* that?"

"A motorcar, I think."

There weren't many in Van Meter, not like in big cities like Cedar Rapids and Des Moines. Here, I could count on one hand the number of folks who'd traded in their carriages for Mr. Ford's noisy new contraption.

But it seemed that one of them was coming—now.

Moments later, I spotted it: a two-seater Model A runabout, its lights shining on approach.

"Who is it?" Alex asked me. "Can you tell?"

"Mr. Griffith. Probably back from a sales run."

Ulysses G. Griffith, together with his brother David, owned Griffith Brothers Implement, hawking wares that ranged from farming tools to seed. Though a young man, he was rich enough to never grant me a second glance, except maybe to wonder why I was on the street at this hour with the town's pretty blind girl.

Instinctively, I tucked Alex behind me. She didn't protest. She knew my reputation and understood that I was likely to be jailed or even whipped if someone witnessed me "sniffing around" Alexandra Harrer. And she further knew that anything she, herself, might say in my defense would fall on stone ears.

Begger. Son of the town drunk.

So, with my dream girl at least partially concealed, I watched Griffith and his "horseless carriage" trundle by.

Fortunately, Mr. Griffith, wearing a long coat, wool hat, and motorman's goggles, seemed to have fixed his attention on something further down Main Street.

Curious, I looked where he was looking.

"What the Sam Hill?" I muttered.

Still tucked close behind me, Alex demanded, "What is it?"

"There's a light," I replied.

And there was. It shone from atop a building a block east of here. At first, I mistook it for the moon, but tonight there wasn't one. Besides, this was brighter than that. What's more, it seemed to be moving, sliding along the roof of Mather and Gregg's, one of the taller businesses in town. Brighter than any lantern, but too white to be fire.

"Hank Trotter!" Alex exclaimed. "Ain't you gonna tell me what you're looking at?"

"Try that again," I told her smugly. "Poor English."

She smacked my calf with her cane, using it like one of Pop's switches.

"Ow!"

"What do you see?" she demanded.

"There's a bright light on top of a building."

"Is it moving?"

"Yeah. Back and forth a bit. I don't know what it is."

Alex said nothing.

A block past us now, I could just make out Griffith leaning forward and peering up at the light. I expected him to brake to a stop, but he never did, though his motorcar's advance slowed to a crawl.

Then, without warning, the light atop Mather and Gregg's winked out.

I gasped.

"What?" Alex demanded.

"It's gone!"

Again, she said nothing.

Around us, the night remained quiet. Even Mr. Griffith's noisy Ford sounded muted and far away.

I felt the hairs on the back of my neck stand up.

Seconds passed.

Suddenly, the light reappeared, this time atop a roof across the street from its initial location. Distantly, I heard Griffith utter a particularly bawdy oath. The church ladies would have been scandalized.

"What's he doing?" Alex asked.

"It's on a different roof."

"No. What's *Mr. Griffith* doing?"

"Oh, he's just driving by it. But slow, real slow."

"He's not stopping?"

"No. At least, not yet."

"Good," she said. "Then maybe we can still—"

The light winked out a second time. No fading. No shuttering to suggest an oil lantern or some such thing. One instant there, and then next—

"Gone!" I declared.

"Wait."

I waited. A minute passed, then two. Nothing. After five or so, I figured whatever it was must be done for the night. Mr. Griffith apparently thought the same, because his Ford sped up, carrying him further down Main toward his home.

My mouth felt dry.

Slowly, I turned to Alex. Even in the poor light, I could tell she was still crying. "I missed her."

"Missed who?"

"I'm sorry, Hank."

"Al... you ain't making a bit of sense."

For once, she didn't correct my grammar. "I know. Please... be patient with me. I think I'm going to need your help for what's coming."

"What *is* coming?" I asked her.

"Will you help me?"

Gazing down at her, I almost blurted, *"I'd do anything for you."* But wearing that much heart on my sleeve scared me. I *was* the town beggar after all, and certainly not what a girl like Alexandra Harrer wanted.

"You know where I'll be," I told her. "If you need me, come get me. And if you just, you know, what to talk about this, I'm here for you."

Then Alex did something she'd never done before. She went up on her toes and, with that weird accuracy of hers, kissed my cheek.

It was a simple gesture. But it almost set me on fire.

If Alex noticed, however, she didn't let on.

That morning found the good people of Van Meter, if not quite "agog" yet, then certainly intrigued by Mr. Griffith's story.

Given how fast it had spread, I guessed that the salesman had told his tale pretty liberally. During the hours before midday, with Alex and the other town kids at school, it was all I heard about. As I said, I didn't go to school. The whole business had always seemed like a waste of time to my pop; it was one of the few things we'd ever agreed on. In truth, however, in the last eight months Alexandra Harrer had become my school.

I didn't understand why she'd taken such a shine to the local beggar. But she'd been new in town and friendless, so maybe that was the whole of it right there. But I'd never asked her. Don't look a gift horse in the mouth. Another thing my pop and I agreed on.

Anyway, sitting on Main Street that morning with my usual hat in my hand, discussion of Mr. Griffith's sighting was everywhere. Mrs. Waverly, whose husband sat on the Village Counsel with Mr. Griffith himself, chatted with other church ladies close to where I sat with my back against the bakery frontage. "It'll be in the newspaper by noon," she insisted.

To which another church lady remarked, "Poor Ulysses must be beside himself!"

"Well," a third one said. "If a good Christian man says he saw strange lights on rooftops, then he did."

"Still..." remarked yet another. "Such a mystery." Then she dropped a penny in my hat as absently as you might pet a dog, and the four of them sauntered away without offering me so much as eye-contact, never mind a "good morning."

But I was used to such things.

Besides, that church lady hadn't been wrong. Last night *was* a mystery, one that nagged at me.

After all our past-midnight business, Alex had left me on the roadside with that hasty goodnight kiss. No explanation. No promise of an explanation. Just the *tap, tap* of her cane as she'd headed off in the direction of her aunt's big house. At the time, I'd merely been sorry to see her go, especially given that cheek kiss. But now, in broad daylight and engrossed in my usual "routine," I found myself fretting over it.

Alex's aunt was Moira Van Meter, whose grandfather had been one of the area's first settlers and source of the town's name. Moira had never married, but she was certainly rich, old money rich, and she occupied a three-story ranch house at Van Meter's northern edge. It was just herself, a cook, a cleaning girl, and Alexandra, who slept in a room beneath the eaves. I'd never been there, of course. Moira Van Meter would never allow the likes of me to enter her family home. But Alex had frequently told me how she enjoyed sleeping in her little "cave" at the top of the house.

Now, however, it left me pondering. Though she hadn't said so last night, she must surely have left her "cave" in the midnight hours, only to then sneak down two floors and out a door without waking the household.

Quite the trick for a blind girl.

I'd have to ask her about it when school was dismissed at 3:00. But, between now and then, all I could do was beg and kill time.

I actually did reasonably well that morning. Ten pennies. It was enough to let me eat for the day, and maybe tomorrow too, if I was careful. Around noon, I went down to the grocery where I bought a loaf of bread, a pickle, and a bit of cheese, all of which I ate right outside on the street. Then I carefully split the remaining coins between my pocket and my sock, replaced my hat on my head—and reluctantly went home.

The Trotter abode occupied a weedy lot on the western side of town, a mile from the creek, the brick factory, and the abandoned coal mine. Not much bigger than Old Mary Durbin's shed, it was just a single room wrapped in a drafty clapboard shell. Here, my pop, a former coal miner, had raised me—if you can call it that—after my mom died when I was in diapers. For the first five years of my life, that shack was all I knew.

It wasn't until Deputy Dormer knocked on our door one memorable Tuesday and cited some state law about all children attending primary school that I first glimpsed how big the world really was—even if that glimpse was just of Van Meter, Iowa.

My father took to my new schooling even less than I did. Having me gone five days a week quickly turned him sour, a sourness that, of course, he took out on me. I got beaten for not doing my homework. I also got beaten for *doing* my homework, especially if Pop thought it was making me "uppity like the rest of them"—and especially when he'd been hitting his bottle.

For a while, I'd thought that old brown bottle was magic. No matter how much he drank, it never seemed to empty. Later, I learned that every few nights he went to Dawson's Bar and refilled it from the supply of "cheap stuff" that Frank Dawson kept in the back room.

So much for magic.

Of course, that was before the mine closed, and Pop lost his job and what little liquor money he had.

These days, his sole means of refilling that brown bottle was *me*.

I opened the shack's only door slowly. If Pop was sleeping, as he often did late into the morning, the last thing I wanted to do was wake him.

Sadly, he wasn't sleeping.

"Boy!" he snapped. It was his usual monicker for me. I sometimes wondered if he remembered my name.

"Hi, Pop," I said, my heart sinking.

"Ain't seen you in two days."

"Sorry, Pop."

"Empty your pockets." He wore a familiar, rheumy glare filled with accusation. I knew better than to meet it squarely. The way his hands twitched as he sat at the old, rickety table—well, it was crystal clear that he ached to hit something, or somebody.

I went to him, head down, and emptied my pockets onto the tabletop. He regarded the coins, licking his lips greedily.

"That all of it?"

I nodded.

"You lying to me, boy?"

"No, Pop."

"Maybe a search would say something different."

It wouldn't. The money from my sock was wrapped in cheesecloth and tucked safely away in a particular tree stump a quarter mile down the road. I'd been handling things that way for six months, ever since Alex had suggested it. Every day, I kept twenty-five percent of my beggings.

Never more than that though. I didn't need my pop any more suspicious than he already was.

"It's early," he said, counting the money. "Why'd you come back so early."

"Need fresh clothes," I replied, head still down. "Folks were saying I stink."

He nodded. "You do. Get the clothes. Then go down to the creek and clean your sorry ass. After that, I want you back out there, hat in hand. I gave you life, you little shit, and you owe me more than this pittance."

"Okay, Pop," I replied.

"You been hanging around that Harrer girl again, I hear."

"No, Pop," I said.

I could feel him scowling, knowing the lie. "That right? Well, Dormer came. He said that you ain't been in school, which I don't give two shits about. But he also said that late last night, the feed man Griffith drove by you and some girl on Main Street who looked a lot like that blindy."

"It wasn't me," I said, studying my feet.

I heard the chair scrape and tensed myself, expecting a slap or even a fist. It didn't come. In fact, when I risked a peek, Pop hadn't even stood up. Maybe he was too tired, or too drunk, to bother. "Better not be… 'cause Dormer said he'll arrest you if he catches you with her. She's a proper girl and you're… well, you."

"Okay, Pop," I said.

"You're no good to me in county jail, boy. With my back, you know I can't work for myself. That means you owe me. You owe me everything."

"Yes, Pop."

"Get out of here, then. Forget that blind girl and focus on sticking your hand out. Come back with this little again and maybe I'll take one of your fingers. Bet that'd muster up some sympathy from the high and mighties. You hear me, boy?"

"Yeah, Pop."

Without another word spoken, I left the ramshackle hovel that hadn't been a home to me in a long time. Pop would spend what I'd given him quickly. By the time I returned this evening, he'd be drunk and wouldn't even notice when I dropped his share on the table and disappeared again—back to Mary Dubin's rundown old shed.

Back to Alex.

I'd long ago stopped hoping the old man—he was barely forty—would spend what I gave him on food instead of cheap liquor. Instead, I figured I'd come by during one of these "visits" and find him dead, either on his bed or slumped in the rickety outhouse. God knows I didn't wish for it. But I *did* figure it.

I felt dejected as I headed down to the creek. Pop's warning about Alex wasn't anything new, I'd been hearing it ever since she and I had become friends not long after she'd appeared in Van Meter. Most of the town kids shied away from her. A blind girl, after all, wasn't very good for games, and she kept too much to herself for any of the "proper" boys to hold hope of stealing a kiss. Not that I blamed them for trying.

God knew *I* dreamed about kissing her.

But, in my heart of hearts, I knew it would never happen.

Except… last night it did.

True, it was just my cheek and only for a second, the gesture likely more about gratitude than, well, anything else. But a kiss was a kiss, and I swore I could still feel the softness of it on the skin beside my nose.

I reached Bulgar Creek, a quiet spot in the woods close to where it spilled into the Raccoon River outside of town. Pop had told me to wash, and he'd been right. I always got more alms when I didn't smell like a month of sweat. But, dang it all, I didn't want to wash off that kiss!

It was a foolish notion, but I felt it anyhow.

Resignedly, I removed my shirt and trousers, rinsed them in the cold water, and then spread them on out a rock to dry in the midday sun. Then I slipped into the creek myself, the water about hip deep this time of year, and started working on my armpits and nether regions. I had no soap. Instead, I counted on friction to get off the worst of the grime.

And, all the while, I thought about last night.

What was *that light?*

It had been brighter than the moon. No wonder Mr. Griffith was captivated—so captivated, in fact, that I'd dared hope he hadn't noticed Alex and me on the roadside. But my luck, as usual, had failed me.

Still, the question begged.

What had *been on that rooftop?*

Then: *Alex knows.*

That thought, which had been nibbling at my edges all morning, now jumped front and center. Of course, she knew. That light, or whatever had made it, was why she'd snuck out in the middle of the night, made her way across town, and woken me in the shed.

Yes, indeed. Blind little Alex Harrer, who couldn't see the light, knew full well what it was.

She just hadn't trusted me enough to tell me.

I didn't see Alex at all that day.

That afternoon, I returned to Main Street, moving from spot to spot with the shade and drawing in some pretty good coin. People were talking, you see, and talking people tend to be freer with their purses. Don't ask me why, but they are.

I even came within earshot of Mr. Griffith, himself. Frankly, if the teller of that tale of lights on rooftops had been almost anyone other than this young, handsome salesman, I don't believe the church ladies would have been quite so supportive. But listening to him recount it for what must have been, for him, the hundredth time, I could see from the faces of his rapt audience that he'd won both their hearts and minds.

"I can't say for sure what it was, ladies," Griffith declared as he stood outside the feed shop, just half a block from where the light had first appeared. "But no one can tell me it was of this world. I swear to it as a sober Christian."

Trust me, the church ladies *loved* that.

Then he absently dropped a nickel in my hat. A whole nickel!

When I stopped back at home that evening, the shack stood empty. Pop was out somewhere, likely refilling his brown bottle, and that was just fine. I slipped his share of my afternoon's beggings under his worn straw pillow—"Outta sight, boy. I don't trust nobodyin this town." Afterward, and for no particular reason, I peeked under the bed.

The box was there, same as always. His secret. His revenge.

And I knew what was inside it, too.

I quietly left.

I went back to what I'd already come to think of as "my shed," and settled down for the night. Waiting there for me, I had a lamp, a book, some stale bread, and an old milk bottle filled with stream water. My typical supper.

The book was, as always, a loaner from Alex. *"When Knighthood Was a Flower"* by Edwin Caskoden, though Alex had informed me that this was a *non de plume*, or a pen name, for Charles Major. At the time, I'd remarked that since I didn't know who either Caskoden or Major was, all that fuss to hide the author's identity seemed foolish. For some reason, Alex had found that observation funny. I hadn't understood why then, but I did now.

Ignorance *could* be funny, though not necessarily in a nice way.

Alex was so much smarter than me.

The book's story was okay, more romance than action, despite the title. But it filled a couple of hours before exhaustion got the better of me. As I lay my head on the straw, I felt sad, though if asked, I couldn't have said why. Or, perhaps more honestly, I couldn't have *admitted* why, not even to myself.

Love can have sharp edges.

And sometimes, they cut you.

Chapter Two

This time, when my dream girl came for me, I wasn't dreaming. I wasn't even sleeping. Instead, I lay awake in the dark shed, surrounded by the smell of moldy wood. When the door creaked open, I didn't move. Instead, I listened to her footfalls and the *tap* of her cane as she made her way unerringly toward me. I hadn't known any other blind people, but something told me that Alex was somehow less blind than she let on. Not that she could actually *see*, mind you. I'd watched her interact with the world too much to ever believe that.

But there was definitely something — more

"Hank," she whispered, nudging my leg with her cane.

"I'm awake."

"Oh!" She sounded surprised. "I… uh… need your help again."

"What for?"

"I'll tell you on the way."

"You'll tell me now, or I ain't going."

"Hank, please…"

I sat up and lit the lantern. "What was that light last night, Al?"

She visibly swallowed. "I… can't tell you that."

"Why not?"

I expected her to get angry. Alex had a temper, and nothing stoked it like someone pushing her into a corner. I'd seen it, most notably behind the schoolhouse, when a local girl had tried on the bully hat. She'd snatched away Alex's cane and, laughing, had pantomimed tapping it on the ground while at the same time feeling the air ridiculously with her other hand.

Alex had punched her dead in the eye, knocking her down and sending her home crying. When the teacher and the girl's parents had shown up at Moira's mansion the next day, Alex had simply said she'd been trying to get her cane back. How could a blind girl, after all, punch someone in the eye so unerringly?

Later on, though, she told me she'd simply followed the sound of the girl's laughter.

That anger had never been turned on me. The worst I'd ever suffered was a kind of annoyed disappointment, usually deserved, like when I promised to write something for her and didn't deliver.

Nevertheless, I was prepared for anger.

Instead, I got tears.

And—well, that just wasn't fair.

She dropped down onto the straw beside me, water flowing from her sightless eyes. My wall of indignation collapsed as if made of feathers and I took her hand without even thinking about it. "I'm in trouble, Hank." Her words were wrapped in sobs. I'd never seen her like this before and it scared me—badly.

"Please tell me what's going on," I begged. "I'll help you."

"If I do, you won't be my friend anymore."

"Alexandra Harrer, I'll be your friend until the end of the world."

She squeezed my hand, her head bowed. Then she said softly, "Someone's come looking for me."

"Someone? Who?"

"I… can't."

"Does this someone want to… hurt you?" Just saying it made my blood boil.

"No!" she replied at once. "But if I don't find them, then *they're* the one who'll get hurt."

That made no sense at all. But she was holding my hand, which she rarely did, even being blind and all. What's more, she'd never opened up like this before, and I wanted it to keep going. "And that's who made that light last night?"

She nodded.

"And you think they're out again tonight, looking for you."

She nodded again, wiping her eyes with her free hand.

"I don't understand. Why doesn't this person just ask around town?"

That only made her start crying again.

"Okay, okay," I said quickly. "Forget that. If you gotta find them in the middle of the night, then that's what we'll do."

"Have to," she said between snuffles, correcting my grammar again.

I sighed. "Have to."

By the time we returned to Main Street, we'd stopped holding hands. I missed it. I know that sounds maudlin. But, all the way into town, I found myself keenly aware of the space between my fingers.

Like I said: love is sharp.

Main Street was quiet, with no motorcars and every rooftop dark under an overcast sky.

"Do you see anything?" Alex asked urgently.

"No," I replied. "It's almost pitch dark. I brought my lantern. Maybe I could... signal them?"

A northern breeze stirred the dry fall leaves blanketing the street.

A chill rolled down my back, one that I couldn't completely credit to the cold.

Something's out here with us.

"Do that," Alex finally said. "But Hank, if you see her, don't be scared. I promise she won't hurt you."

"She?"

No reply.

I lit the lantern using one of my three remaining matches and held it high. On a night as dark as this, it would be visible from any of the rooftops.

"It's lit," I reported. My mouth had gone dry.

"If she's here, she'll see it," Alex told me.

Again..." she."

"Al," I said carefully. "Who—"

A bright light flashed into being on a rooftop across the street. Seeing it made my breath catch.

Without me needing to say a word, Alex gasped. "She's here!"

As I watched, the light moved to the roof's edge then sort of jumped off. It floated down with surprising grace, casting its illumination across a dozen storefront windows.

I stared at it, trying to make sense of what I was seeing.

Whatever-It-Was landed in the street with a soft, muted *thump*. Now the light was pointing straight at us, maybe fifty feet away and seven or eight feet above the road. I got the impression of a shape behind that light, two legs and a long body.

What on Earth am I looking at?

Beside me, Alex's face split into a broad, relieved smile. The cane fell from her grasp, something that never happened, and she started forward, spreading her arms as if intending to scoop Whatever-It-Was into them.

My uneasiness turned into naked alarm. Instinctively, I reached for her. "Alex, wait!"

But she didn't. Instead, her walk turned into a run as she neared the light—and the *thing* that was casting it.

My heart in my throat, I started after her, dropping the lantern and not giving it a second thought as its wick drowned in oil and winked out. Now, Alex could be quick when she wanted, but my legs were longer than hers and, with luck, I'd catch the girl before the girl caught the—whatever.

Then, as it often does, fate stepped in and mucked the whole thing up.

A storefront door opened up ahead, close to the light and almost abreast with Alex. A figure emerged, blinking in the unlikely glare. It was a slightly built man in trousers and a white long-sleeve shirt with its tail out. His dark hair was tousled, as if he'd been roused from sleep which, given the hour, he surely had.

But all those details disappeared when I saw the gun.

It was a *big* one, a six-shot revolver that looked almost as long as my forearm. The man held it in one trembling hand and, his eyes wild with fear, pointed it at the *thing* that stood no more than fifteen feet away from him.

A sighted person might have stopped in time. Alex didn't. She slammed into the man's back, knocking him two steps forward before bouncing off him and landing hard on her buttocks in the dusty street. The man uttered a frightened cry and started to turn, that monstrous gun still shaking in his fist.

This whole thing was going from bad to worse.

"Wait!" I cried. "She's blind! She can't see you!"

In that instant, the light changed its angle, for the first time allowing me, allowing all of us, to really see what was behind it.

"Oh… my… God…" somebody whispered. To this day, I'm not sure if it was me or the man with the gun.

It stood eight feet tall, a lean leathery-skinned body atop long muscular legs that ended in three-toed claws for feet. Instead of arms, it had wings. These were folded back and tucked in close so that the creature—and, make no mistake, it was a "creature" and not any kind of man or animal—could lean its weight on what passed for elbows. It had a long, slender neck atop muscled shoulders and a strangely elongated head, a bit like that of a horse, but with a sharp beak jutting out from between two small black eyes.

Above all that, about where its forehead was or should be, was a blunt, fist-sized horn. And it was this, somehow *this*, that cast a bright light over half of Main Street.

The man with the gun screamed. Then he raised his hand cannon— and fired.

Except, he didn't.

Instead, he yelled, "Bang!"

I blinked, my thoughts turning to mud. I glanced down at Alex, who was still on her buttocks maybe ten feet ahead of me. She didn't seem hurt. But neither was she getting herself up. Instead, she waved her hand at the gunman, back and forth, almost as if she were trying to fan him.

The man called "bang!" a second time.

The creature flinched, moving its head to and fro, the light so bright that, when it hit me full in the face, I staggered and had to shield my eyes.

"Bang!" the gunman declared.

The creature turned away, not so much walking along the dusty street as hopping, the way a pigeon might. It seemed more confused than alarmed, its long head with its searchlight still scanning the street.

The man uttered a fourth "bang" and then a fifth.

And that's when the creature took to the air.

The gunman and I both watched with the kind of naked, wide-eyed, slack-jawed incomprehension usually reserved for five-year-olds visiting Santa at the Five and Dime. Wonder. Astonishment. And, yes, some fear.

The creature extended its wings so smoothly that the movement seemed almost balletic. Its clumsy, ungainly hopping was over as those wings began beating with enough force to blow up plumes of road dust.

And on a level not quite conscious, I understood that this was a creature of the air, not the earth.

Then it was gone, swallowed up by the night, its horn light extinguished and the sound of its wing beats fading behind the cold September breeze.

I stared after it, my eyes so wide I wasn't sure I'd ever be able to close them again. Slowly, awareness returned. With enormous effort, I dropped my gaze to the roadside, where Alex was finally finding her feet. She stood now directly behind the gunman, who'd lowered his weapon and was now, as I had been, staring skyward.

For the first time, I recognized him. It was Dr. Alcott, who kept his medical practice right here and, apparently, slept there sometimes as well. The big gun that he hadn't fired now hung at his side, looking so heavy that I was afraid he might drop it. I opened my mouth to say something. But then I noticed Alex. She'd stepped closer to him, her hand still flapping the air. It was a strange gesture, but much more graceful than the way I'm describing it.

If Dr. Alcott noticed, he gave no sign. In fact, I didn't think he'd ever truly realized we were there. After several moments, he sighed wearily. Then, without a word, he stepped back through the open door of his practice and shut it behind him.

Alex, her hand no longer flapping, let out a sigh of her own and looked back at me with such dismay that my heart immediately went out to her.

"I'm sorry, Hank," she said.

I blinked. "For what?"

Then, looking genuinely sorrowful, she flapped her hand at *me*.

I smelled — something.

It's hard to explain. It wasn't a bad smell or even a particularly strong one, but it seemed to fill my brain, fogging over my thoughts. I remember swaying on my feet, the memory of what I'd seen burned into me like a cattle brand. And the next—

—I was back on my straw in Mary Durbin's shed with the morning's light squeezing between the weathered boards.

Crazy dream.

And I kept right on believing that until I headed into town for the morning's beggary.

There, I found the local doctor, Fred Alcott, holding court in front of his storefront practice.

"Eight feet tall, friends! I swear it on my life! Half-human and half-animal, with bat-like wings and a devil's horn atop its head that all but blinded me with its brightness!"

Now, I didn't know the doctor well. He'd never spoken to me, and I'd never had the money to see him no matter how sick I got. So it surprised me to see him talking this way, addressing the gathered townsfolk the way a carpetbagger might. "I tell you all, it could have come from nowhere but the deepest pits of Hell!"

I watched from a nearby corner, studying his listeners' rapt faces. A few church ladies even swayed on their feet, as if the tale were nearly too harrowing to bear. But they all applauded as the good doctor recounted firing on the beast not less than five times. "But my shots were wasted, as the bullets had no effect other than to chase it away from me, my neighbors, and my town!"

"Bang," I thought, remembering my dream.

Was it possible for two people to have the same dream? And, if it *wasn't* a dream, how was it that the doctor knew that when I hadn't.

That was when the heavy hand fell on my shoulder. Now there weren't too many people in Van Meter who would freely touch me.

In fact, I could only name two. One was Alex.

"Henry Trotter," Deputy Lucas Dormer said. "I was hoping to run into you this morning."

Dormer was a big man of about thirty-five years with a smooth face and shaved head. He wore his Sheriff's Department uniform as though born into it, the badge on his chest polished to a mirror shine. His big, blunt fingers dug into my shoulder, keeping me from bolting. And I *would* have, given the chance. Meeting up with the law was rarely a good start to my day.

"Got some questions for you, Henry," he said, smiling without smiling. "Can you spare a moment in your busy schedule?"

"Sure," I replied. What else could I say? Backtalking would likely get me slapped, or worse.

Dormer's eyes, blue like Alex's but cold where hers were warm, flicked up to the ladies and their hero of the moment. "Let's head over to my office. No need to bother these good folks, is there?"

I didn't reply. I didn't have to. It hadn't been a request.

He didn't shackle me, which was a small blessing. It implied that he didn't think I'd done anything, which I hadn't. This *had* to be about last night. Maybe Alcott had told him Alex and I were there. Maybe he just wanted to get my side of things without indulging the gossip-mongers any further. By now, it seemed clear to me that what happened last night hadn't been a dream—though, on my life, I couldn't remember anything after Alex said, "I'm so sorry, Hank."

What Deputy Dormer called his office was simply Van Meter's branch of the Dallas County Sheriff's Department. Most of the time, Luke Dormer was our sole lawman. Crime was rare in Van Meter, outside of a few drunk and disorders, truancies, or juvenile vandalism situations. Oh, and vagrancy, of course—as in my case. My pop was the town drunk, and I was the illiterate beggar-boy who slept in folks' stables or barns more often than under his worthless fathers' leaky roof. True, I didn't break laws outside some harmless trespassing. But, as Pop liked to say, trouble is as trouble does.

And so, Dormer kept his eye on me.

"Sit," he told me when we got to the jail. There was only one cell in the small building just off Main Street, and it was currently unoccupied. I'd visited it over the years and knew from bitter experience just how many bed bugs lived in its bunk mattress. That made me perfectly glad to settle for a rickety wooden chair, so long as it was on *this* side of those bars.

I expected the deputy to sit behind his desk. But instead, he stood over me—Alex would probably want me to write "loomed" for its dramatic effect—his big hands on his hips.

"Henry," he said, his expression hard. "I'm going to ask this once. Just once."

I nodded.

"Where is Alexandra Harrer?"

I blinked. "What?"

The cuff he gave me was hard enough to almost knock me to the floor. The whole left side of my face caught fire. I yelled out a pretty nasty curse, which put a smirk on the deputy's face. While I rubbed my cheek, he leaned down close. "Seems she left her room last night, sometime after midnight, and never came back. Her Aunt Moira, Mrs. Van Meter, is beside herself with worry. I've been there most of the morning. Doesn't look like there was any kind of break in or struggle, which makes me think the girl… a blind girl… left of her own accord. Now, why would she do that, Henry?"

I stared up at him, dumbfounded.

Alex.

My only friend was missing, and had been since she'd been with me in that dream that wasn't a dream.

My mind struggled to process it all, trying to line up the pieces and make them fit.

"I asked you a question!" Dormer barked. "Where's Alexandra Harrer?"

"I don't know!" I exclaimed.

He cuffed me again, just as hard, same cheek. "Let me see if I can guess." The words came out in a hiss. "You forced yourself on her, didn't you? You're in love with her, the whole town knows that! And when you finally confessed it, she spurned you, didn't she, Romeo? You got mad and—"

"No!" I screamed, tears in my eyes. "I'd kill myself before I'd hurt her!"

"Then what did you do with her?"

"I haven't seen her since last night!"

Dormer grabbed my shirt and pulled me to my feet. "Last night? What about last night?"

"We were there!" I cried, hating the way my voice broke. "On Main Street when that monster showed up!"

That gave him pause. "Monster. You mean that yarn Fred Alcott's been spinning all morning?"

I nodded, snot running from my nose. Wherever Alex was, I thanked God Almighty she couldn't see me now.

The deputy got a thoughtful, faraway look in his eyes. Then, apparently deciding that, monster or not, he had to focus on the matter at hand, his eyebrows knit, and he glared at me anew. "Forget all that. What happened after? Where did you and Alex go?"

This was the part I knew he wouldn't believe. More likely than not, I'd get cuffed a third time and probably lose a tooth in the process. But there wasn't any lie I could think of that would serve me any better. "I… don't know. Something happened after the monster left. Alex told me… she said she was sorry and the next thing I knew I woke up sleeping in Mary Dubin's shed."

"How'd you get there?"

"I don't know."

"Did you walk?"

"I don't remember walking."

"Well, that slip of the blind girl sure didn't carry you."

I said nothing. He was right about that.

He let go of me. I stood there, trembling and rubbing at my face. "Deputy, I swear to you, I don't know where Alex is… but I hope to God she's okay."

"I thought you two were friends."

"We're… something. I used to think it was friends. But lately, I'm not so sure."

"What's that mean?"

I shrugged. "It's easy to like a stray dog when it licks your hand."

The deputy seemed to consider that. When he looked at me again, it was with less heat. "Okay, Henry. I believe you. I've known you your whole life, and I don't think you have it in you to hurt anybody, much less that poor blind girl. Sorry I hit you, but I had to be sure."

I didn't respond. I mean, what do you say to a thing like that? Thanks?

But Dormer wasn't finished. "Makes me wonder about your dad, though."

"My…" I began, but the word trailed off.

He nodded. "I've known him a long time, too. And he's got a temper. I've talked to him more than once about your… association… with the Harrer girl. He doesn't much care for it."

"My pop doesn't much care for anything that doesn't involve me begging for him."

Dormer nodded, as if this glimpse into the inner workings of the Trotter family was something he both already knew and didn't much care about. "Do you think he might have done something about it?"

"You mean about… Alex?"

"That's what I mean."

It wasn't something I'd ever considered. Sure, Pop didn't like me passing time with the local rich girl, blind or otherwise. He thought it might get me into trouble, which would then keep me from funding his bottle. But *do something about it*?

Was Dormer asking if my father would *hurt* Alex to get her out of my life? That was just crazy.

Wasn't it?

"No," I said. "I can't see him every doing a thing like that."

The deputy chewed on this and, from his expression, didn't much like the taste of it. "Well, blind girls don't wander off on their own. That means *somebody* did *something*. Now, a few folks are saying this 'monster' everybody's talking about took her. But I don't believe in monsters. So, if it wasn't you and you don't figure it was your dad, then I'm in a bit of a pickle, aren't I?"

I didn't answer. I might not have been as smart as Alex, but I could see where this was going. I could imagine the townsfolk gathering under Moira Van Meter's banner, calling for someone — anyone — to pay for their missing princess. And who better than the son of the town ne'er-do-well, a panhandler and grubby truant vagabond. Dormer's message was simple enough: if Alexandra Harrer didn't reappear soon, then I could expect my future to get very bleak indeed.

Yet, as worrisome as that was — and it was worrisome — it paled beside the much more immediate question.

Where had my dream girl gone?

Dormer let me go. I wasn't at all sure he would and, frankly, felt no small surprise when he did. Regardless, as I stepped out into the overcast fall day, he left me with this bit of advice: "Find her, Henry. I'll be looking too, as will others. But you know her, maybe better than anyone, including her aunt. Go search out the places you know she likes, not in town but outside of it. Find her, boy. For her sake and yours."

I nodded. And that was that.

I searched.

I checked her favorite spots along the creek. She wasn't there. I checked the field across from her aunt's stables. Alex loved horses, though they tended to get agitated around her. Despite that, she would often loiter near them, which always confused me. What could a blind girl get out of being close to animals that disliked her?

But again, she wasn't there.

If I hadn't been warned to stay out of town, I'd have checked the candy shop and general store, two of Alex's favorite haunts. But if she'd gone to either of those places, Dormer would have already found her.

As morning became afternoon, I went further afield, relying more on desperate hunches than any real hope. But Alex was nowhere to be found. Finally, and with no small reluctance, I went home. I didn't think my father would have hurt Alex. Heck, I wasn't sure he even knew what she looked like. But Dormer's suspicions nagged at me, like an itch I couldn't quite reach, and so I went.

It didn't go well.

From the moment, I stepped through the shack's only door, the old man was on me.

"Where the hell you been?" he demanded, advancing like a mad bear. It wasn't yet two in the afternoon, but I could smell the liquor on him. His eyes took on a wild, dangerous cast whenever he'd decided to forgo food for drink. And right now that poison was churning inside him, turning impatience into anger, frustration into anger and, worst of all, self-loathing into anger.

Before I could answer his question, he hit me. It wasn't one of Dormer's hard slaps, either, but a full-on punch to my face. I flinched at the last second. If I hadn't, he'd have broken my nose. As it was, his blow glanced off my temple, which was enough to make me stagger and see stars. I tried to put some space between us, but the closed door was at my back.

He screamed, "You were supposed to be here by noon with my money! I ain't eaten anything since yesterday!"

He threw another fist, a big roundhouse. But drink spoiled his aim and, when I ducked, he hit the door—hard. With a yowl, he pulled back, promptly tripped on his own feet, and hit the dirt floor hard enough to knock the wind out of himself.

For a few long seconds, I stood over him, my own breath coming in heaves. He gasped and flopped like a landed fish, cradling his fist. Glancing at the door, I saw blood on the wood.

My pop had probably just broken his hand.

I tried to muster up some sympathy. But it was hard. My vision still swam a little from his first hit.

"Where's Alex?" I heard myself say.

When he didn't answer, I leaned over. "Did you do something to Alexandra Harrer?"

Watching him like this, drunk and breathless and in pain, should have gnawed at my conscience. But there'd been so many punches, so many outright beatings, that—awful as it sounds—pity for the man who'd sired me seemed in short supply.

But my words got through his fog of liquor because he looked blearily up at me and asked, "W… what?"

"Alex," I said. "My friend. My *only* friend in this world. Did you do something to her?"

I watched him suck down in a lungful of air. "What're you jawing about, boy?" he finally replied. "I ain't seen that rich girl! I don't think I'd know her if I did."

This sounded so much like my own reasoning a few minutes ago that I sensed truth in it. With a tired sigh, I straightened and went to the door. "Wait..." he gasped, sounding just piteous enough to make me look questioningly back at him. "You got money, boy?"

"No," I replied, which was true. "And I'm done giving you any when I get some," I added, which was also true, though I hadn't realized it until that very moment.

"You owe me!" he snarled, still clutching his ruined hand. "We're kin! I'm your father!"

"You stopped being any kind of father to me when you decided rearing me meant beating me half to death."

"I got that right!"

"Not no more you don't. I'm done with you." Another thing I'd just now realized.

"One more against me!" he wailed. "You're just like the rest! Don't forget what I took from the mine when they put me out like trash! Don't forget what I could do if I wanted!"

I'd heard this speech before, plenty of times. I knew perfectly well what was in the box under his bed. And I knew perfectly what he could do with it if he felt so inclined.

But if living with a drunk had taught me anything, it was that they weren't exactly self-starters. My old man would never use that box. Of that, I was sure.

When I didn't reply, he cursed me. Not that I stayed to listen. I left that place and didn't look back, letting all that vitriol — Alex would be proud of me for coming up with that one — send me on my way like bitter tailwind.

Of course, I had no home anymore. But that was a worry for later.

Right now, I still had a dream girl to find.

Except I *didn't* find her, not that afternoon and not that evening.

By the time the sun set, though, I had an idea — a long shot, but better than nothing. Unfortunately, this idea of mine presented two problems. The first was patience. I'd become sick with worry and the thought of waiting the necessary hours seemed about as possible as flapping my arms and flying to the moon. The second problem was worse. By now, the townsfolk would be worried too, with Moira Van

Meter leading the pack and, as Deputy Dormer had suggested, the easiest target for their ire was me. Foolishly, I'd told him that I'd been sleeping in Mary Dubin's shed, which made going back there unwise.

I needed to do my waiting where no one would think to look.

With darkness closing in, I arrived at Alex's house, the home of Moira Van Meter.

If it wasn't the biggest abode in town, then it was surely in the running, a fancy two-story farmhouse with six bedrooms, a library, and—according to Alex—a genuine indoor privy. Of course, I'd never risk stepping inside. But there *was* a stable, with only a pair of old mares that Moira kept mainly for infrequent Sunday carriage rides. This late, it'd be empty.

So, there I settled down to wait for one in the morning.

The same time that the creature appeared last night, and the night before that, and—hopefully—tonight.

Because my every instinct assured me that where *it* was, Alex would be, too.

Chapter Three

The hours dragged on in that cold stable. With no book to read nor lamp to read it by, I spent my time replaying first the events of the last two nights and then the whole of my association with Alexandra Harrer.

I hadn't known how lonely I'd been before her first coin dropped into my hat on Main Steet. That had been back in mid-January. She'd asked my name. She'd asked how old I was. She'd talked to me as few townsfolk ever did. She'd stayed with me until her aunt arrived and scolded her for "wasting time." Watching Alex get dragged away, my heart sank. Imagine living your life in darkness and then, finally, glimpsing the sun — only to have it set before you've had time to really understand, much less appreciate it.

Fortunately, the sun came back the next day, and the day after that.

Alex asked me to "show" her Van Meter, not the streets and houses, but the woods and fields and streams. I did this willingly, eagerly, gratefully, and every moment with her was precious as gold. We didn't hold hands, except on rare moments when her cane wasn't enough to guide her across rocky or uneven ground. But, between my ears, I was always touching her. At her urging, I recounted, with no small shame, the sad story of my motherless, illiterate life. And she, with a determination that seemed to belie anything like pity, began the admittedly arduous process of a blind girl teaching a beggar boy how to read. At first, I doubted she could. After all, no one, including my father, had ever accused me of being bright. But she assured me I would learn.

And, over the next few months, learn I did.

Then, after that, she taught me how to *write*.

I'd always loved storytelling. But Alex pushed me to write my stories down, and even brought paper and pencil for me to do just that.

She had me read aloud every word, eventually declaring me a natural "folk author" in the vein of Mark Twain. And, to underline this point, she had me read some of the man's novels. To this day, *A Connecticut Yankee in King Arthur's Court* is my favorite.

She spent at least an hour with me each day, more during the weekends and summers, when school didn't command so much of her time.

Blind since birth, Alex had found herself suddenly orphaned and sent by her family's attorney to live with her mother's sister in Van Meter. Details beyond that, however, she never shared with me. Alexandra was a private soul.

But she was also my friend, and the most precious thing in my life.

And, God help me, I'd always believed she felt at least something like that toward me.

Now, I wasn't so sure.

For Alex, it seemed, kept secrets, and one of them involved an eight-foot-tall, winged monster with a lamp for a forehead.

Well tonight, if luck was on my side, I'd uncover those secrets.

September 30th 1903 turned into October 1st. Now, I carried no watch back then. But live by your wits long enough and you develop a sense for the time of day. So, when that sense told me, subtly but clearly, that midnight had finally come, I abandoned both my memories and Moira's stable, passing right by its sleeping mares. Outside, the Van Meter night felt weirdly *electric*, the way the air sometimes gets right before a thunderstorm. I couldn't have explained it if pressed, but the sense of impending *something* was so strong that it made the hairs on the back of my neck stand up.

I took heart in the feeling, strange though it was.

It made me think that, just maybe, I was right.

And I was.

A half-moon held court in a partly cloudy sky, casting all of Main Street silver-gray as I made my way downtown, trying to look everywhere at once.

Alex wasn't there.

So, I continued along, watching the rooftops, my nerves jangling.

Around me, the air felt chillier than it had the previous two nights. Autumn could be cold in Iowa, and while this autumn was still pretty new, it seemed determined to carry on the legacy of its forebears.

That's pretty good. Alex would probably want me to write that down.

I shook my head, annoyed with myself.

Then I suddenly stopped. By that, I mean not just my feet but my breath and maybe my heart as well.

Something had just passed in front of the half-moon—there and gone in an instant, little more than a flicker of shadow. A second later, I heard an odd sound, a bit like shaking out a sheet in the wind, but slower, rhythmic, and getting louder.

The creature from last night, looking even more terrifying, seemed to float down from the sky, gliding on its massive wings along Main Street, coming in my direction. It touched down almost soundlessly, surprising given its size, coming to a stop no more than ten feet in front of me.

I stood rooted in place, my eyes unblinking.

It regarded me thoughtfully.

Then it made a sound, the first I'd heard from it.

It was—bizarre. Nothing else, be it Man or Nature, had ever produced such a noise—a sort of loud gurgling crow, though I didn't get the impression that the creature was in pain or distress. Nevertheless, its alien aspect should have scared me, even sent me running.

But it didn't.

And I didn't.

Almost without willing it, I reached my hand out toward this impossible thing standing before me.

As if it response, it hopped closer, coming within six feet, then four. Then the creature's big head came down and met my hand.

I petted it.

It uttered another sound, softer than before, reminding me of a lamb's gentle bleat.

I suddenly thought, *Whatever this is… it's no monster.*
This is more like a… visitor.

Aloud, I heard myself say, "Hello… Visitor."

I swear on my life, the creature sighed under my hand.

Without warning, it suddenly drew back, its large, elongated head turning sharply right. Then that odd, blunted horn between its eyes lit up brilliantly, throwing white light through the window of the building right beside us.

The Van Meter Bank.

As it happened, I knew the bank manager fairly well. Clarence Dunn (Peter to his friends, though I never did find out why) was one of the few on Main Street who tolerated my begging outside his establishment, never once calling Dormer to chase me away. Sometimes, Peter even chatted with me — on slow mornings. He was a good soul, one of the few in Van Meter besides Alex to treat me like a person instead of a bug to be scraped off their shoe.

I started to say something to the creature — "stop that," maybe.

But before I had the chance to do so, the bank window exploded.

The sound was deafening, like a cannon. I cried out as broken shards of glass peppered my left arm. I'd only been at the window's edge however, at the very periphery of the blast.

Visitor took it almost full in the face.

After that, a number of things happened all at once.

I fell hard onto the dirt road. A fog of broken awareness — shock, I suppose — turned everything gray and distant. I watched as the creature once again took to wing, uttering another of those weird gurgling sounds. In an instant, it was gone, vanished back into the night as if it had never been there at all.

Slowly, my stunned mind tried to work through what had happened. Somebody had fired a gun through the bank window at the creature. Had it been Peter, staying overnight in the establishment for one reason or another?

Well regardless, I was in enough trouble already, and being found here on the open street when the shooter came out to investigate seemed — imprudent.

I tried to stand, but my ears were ringing, my limbs sluggish and uncooperative. With a groan, I rolled onto my hands and knees and then staggered to my feet.

I was now facing the way I'd come, my back to the shattered window, my head hammering. Gradually, as my senses cleared, I spotted someone in the street about a block away.

It was a slip of a blonde girl.

And she carried a long cane.

"Al?" I whispered.

She came toward me, feeling the ground with the tip of her cane. At the same time, her free hand seemed to be fanning the air as it had last night.

Something hit my nose, familiar and yet completely strange at the same time.

"What's going on?" I heard myself ask.

Then it seemed as if the world got very small and very tight.

And very dark.

This time, I didn't wake up on straw in Mary Durbin's shed, but on a cot surrounded by brick walls and a slitted window too small for a cat to slip through, much less a man. Behind me, I heard voices. So, I rolled over and peered through vertical steel bars at a partial view of Deputy Dormer's office.

The deputy was there, as were Peter Dunn, Ulysses Griffith, and Dr. Alcott—in short, everyone who had seen the creature during its nightly visits to Van Meter.

Everyone, that is, except Alex.

For now, the men were paying me no mind. Instead, they all stood around Dormer's desk, looking down at something atop it.

My arm stung and, holding it up, I found it bandaged from shoulder to wrist. Dr. Alcott's work, no doubt.

"I don't honestly see what good it'll do, Pete." Griffith said.

"It's proof," the bank manager protested. "Proof that I didn't shoot out my front window for no good reason."

"But did you even hit it?" demanded Dr. Alcott, sounding angry, though I wasn't sure at what.

"Did *you*?" Peter replied hotly. "How many times did you say you fired at it, point blank? Five? Six? Lord knows you bragged all over town about it!"

Alcott's face flushed, but he didn't reply.

"There wasn't any blood on the street," Dormer told them. "And nothing that really looked like tracks, either."

"No tracks!" Peter exclaimed, sounding offended. "What do you call *this*?"

"I don't know what this is, Mr. Dunn," the deputy replied.

"It's footprint, damn it!"

"No need for that language here, Pete," Griffith admonished, his tone light and oh-so-agreeable, a salesman's way of talking.

"It's from no animal I ever saw," Dormer said. "Not a bear and not a deer."

"Bigger than both," Alcott remarked with some sulk. "*If* it's the same thing I saw the other night."

Pete rubbed his face with shaking hands. After shooting out his bank's window, I couldn't imagine him going home and getting any sort of decent sleep.

Then again, *I'd* slept—hadn't I?

"I never saw it," he admitted, sounding a little sick. "Just its light, which all but blinded me. Honestly, I figured it had to be some kind of robbery." Then, when the others regarded him, he sheepishly added, "I've rather thought that might be what's been happening all week, first with Ulysses' rooftop light and then with Fred's monster."

"Monsters don't rob banks, Pete," Alcott said dryly.

"Well… maybe I didn't quite believe that part of your story," Peter told him. "At least, not until I found *this* in the morning." He motioned to the thing on the desk. "Sorry, Doc."

Dr. Alcott said nothing.

"I'm still not seeing what good it'll do," the salesman said, rubbing at the back of his neck. "I mean… even if it *is* a footprint, this thing *flies*, right? It's not like we can go into the woods and track it."

"I wish somebody else had seen it," Alcott muttered.

Peter suddenly brightened. "Maybe Hank did. Maybe that's why he fainted the way he did!"

I wasn't at all sure I'd call what had happened to me "fainting."

"Looks like he's awake," Dormer said. "Let's ask him."

The deputy opened my cell door using the keyring from his belt, pulled me to my feet, and wordlessly dragged me back out into the office. There, with one of his big hands almost painfully tight around my unbandaged forearm, he pointed down at the thing that had so captivated the town's elite.

It was, just as Peter had said, a footprint—or, more accurately, some kind of cast of a footprint. Plaster probably, and chalk white.

"Look familiar?" Dr. Alcott asked. Of the four of them, he seemed the least favorably disposed toward me.

It *did* look familiar. In fact, it looked like one of Visitor's three-toed feet, big as life. Reflexively I swallowed, which Dormer, at least, took as a sign of recognition. "Mr. Dunn found you on the street, Henry," he told me.

"Sorry about your arm," Peter said, sounding like he meant it. "I didn't know you were there."

I nodded but didn't reply.

Dormer's voice was hard, "Want to tell me why you *were* there?"

"I was looking for Alex."

"Alex?" Griffith said, his heavy eyebrows knitted. "Alexandra Harrier?"

Again, I nodded.

Dormer asked, "And what made you think she'd be out on Main Street in the middle of the night?"

Staring into the man's hard gaze, I knew I faced a fork in the road. I could tell these men the truth, that the creature was real *and* was somehow connected to Alex, who'd been on hand for every sighting. More than that, she'd done *something* these past two nights, something that had made Dr. Alcott yell "bang" instead of firing and me faint dead away. I could tell them all that. I might, by some miracle, even make them believe me.

But what would that do to my dream girl?

Love's a funny thing. It persists, even in the deep worry that it isn't returned, even in the face of what I think I'll label "ill treatment." It didn't matter how many secrets she kept from me. It didn't matter how much she treated me like a servant or even, as Pop sometimes said, an outright pet. It didn't even matter that she'd disappeared on me, on the whole town but especially *me*, without so much as a word.

It only mattered that I loved her. Period. End of Sentence.

"I guess I was desperate," I said. "Alex and me were together three nights back when the lights showed up on the roofs."

Griffith agreed, not unkindly. "I saw you."

This, of course, I'd already known.

"Anyways," I said. "I spent the day looking for her. I even went to my pop's place and asked him about her."

"And what did he say?" Dormer asked.

"That he ain't seen her. And he was so drunk that I believed him. I don't know where she is, deputy, and that's the plain truth of it."

All of them stared at me. The general mood in the office seemed to ease. Dormer even relaxed his grip a little.

So, I added quickly, "I swear, I was only looking for Alex." I faced Peter. "I'd never rob you, Mr. Dunn."

He actually smiled. "I know that, Hank. But you saw the monster?"

"Yeah, I did."

"Ha!" declared Peter, as if I'd just proved something for him.

Hesitantly, I added, "Except..."

"Except what, Henry?" Dormer asked.

"Well," I said to him, to all of them. "It's not really a monster, is it? I mean... who's it hurt? Who's it even *tried* to hurt?"

"Because I didn't give it a chance!" Alcott replied sharply, defensively.

The others only looked thoughtful. A moment later, Dormer let go of my arm altogether, making me think I might be walking out of here after all.

But then the street door opened—and, seeing who stood there in partial silhouette against the morning light, I knew I wouldn't be going anywhere.

Moira Van Meter wasn't a hair above five feet tall or a minute below seventy. But, for all that, there was a presence to her. She was town royalty, and she knew it. So did the four church ladies who crowded into the deputy's doorway behind her.

Moira face was lean, not heart-shaped like her niece, with small brown eyes instead of big blue ones. Try as I might, I couldn't find the slightest facial resemblance between them. The old woman scowled while she looked around the small office, as though everything she saw displeased her. Then those brown eyes, sharp as knives, locked on me, and I felt my stomach—already painfully empty—clench.

"Why is that boy not in handcuffs?" Moria Van Meter demanded. The four men standing around Deputy Dormer's desk regarded her with expressions ranging from annoyance to concern to—well—cloying.

"Miss Van Meter!" Peter exclaimed, coming forward and offering his hand. "Good morning to you. Please know that my every prayer is for your niece's safe return."

Spoken like a banker to the richest person in town.

Moira ignored him, her angry eyes moving from me to Dormer, who met them with admirable stoicism. Moria Van Meter was known throughout the county to have a glare than could peel paint.

"I asked you a question, Lucas Dormer," she said while silent church ladies filed into the now crowded office behind her. "Why isn't this... urchin... in handcuffs?"

Dormer replied evenly, "Because he's not under arrest, Miss Van Meter."

The church ladies murmured amongst themselves in that way of theirs. Alex sometimes called it "clucking," but to me it always seemed more—*dangerous*—than that.

Moira waved a be-gloved hand at him dismissively before whirling on me. "Where is my niece, boy?"

I tried to answer, but it was like my throat had closed up. She seemed to take my tongue-tied demeanor as an admission of guilt, because she hauled off and slapped me. After all the beatings I'd taken over the years, you'd think the open-handed slap of an old woman half my size wouldn't amount to much—but she nearly knocked me to the floor. As it was, I staggered and might have upended the plaster cast Peter had made, if Dr. Alcott hadn't managed to snatch it up at the last moment.

"Hold on now," Dormer said, stepping between Moira and myself. "There's no call for that."

"No call!" the old woman exclaimed, her voice shrill. Behind her, the church ladies "clucked" that much harder. Moira and I were going to be the talk of the town by lunchtime. "He's been… *sniffing* around her… almost from the day she came under my charge. A poor, orphaned, blind girl, and this… this… *scamp* saw fit to seduce her!"

"No, I didn't!" I yelled, finally finding my voice. "Alex is my *friend*!"

Moira pointed a laced finger at me. "You have no *right* to be her friend! You're the worthless son of a worthless drunk and I told Alexandra that. I told her that so many times! But youth doesn't listen. And now you've taken her somewhere, haven't you? You've… you've *defiled* my niece and now you're hiding her!" Then she raised her hand as if to slap me again. "Or… or… have you done something worse, you filthy wretch?"

Don't ask me where it came from. I'm not, by nature, particularly courageous. But the notion that I would ever "defile" Alex raised my hackles as few things had in my short life. So, almost without thinking, I found myself stiffening my spine and facing down the richest and most powerful person in town.

Something in my demeanor must have given her pause because Moira's hand froze in mid-slap.

When I spoke, it was with more force and commitment than I'd ever mustered before.

"I would die before I hurt Alex, Miss Moira. She's been kind to me in a way no one else ever has, not even my own kin. So, you can hit me all you like, but it won't make me worthy of the hitting."

Her face colored and, for a moment, I thought she might explode like a stick of dynamite. But then she lowered her hand and turned away from me. "Two or three nights this week," she told Dormer, "this… ruffian… has snuck into my home and spirited my niece away. True, he brought her back before morning, on every occasion that is, except two nights ago. I don't care what protestations he makes. He did something to her."

"That true, Henry?" the deputy asked me. Around us, the gentlemen and the church ladies had gone deathly silent. The very walls seemed suddenly to be holding their breath.

"No, sir," I replied. "Alex would meet me after dark, yes. But I never 'spirited her away.' She came to *me*, sought *me* out, every time."

"A blind girl did that?" Moria derided. "Does that ring true with you, deputy?"

For a moment, Dormer fumbled for an answer. Then, Ulysses Griffith said, "I've seen that girl navigate the street after a rainstorm, missing every puddle, every pile of manure, as if that cane of hers could sense the obstacles in her path."

Dr. Alcott added, "Alexandra came into my practice to find a poultice to help with poison ivy. I was busy with patients and asked to her wait. But she simply went up to my medicine shelf and took what she needed, offering me the exact coin for it. I asked her how she did it, being completely blind. She simply smiled and replied that she could smell the poultice."

"That poultice was for me," I said. "I'd got poison ivy down by the creek and I thought the itching would drive me insane. Alex offered to buy me something to help. I didn't want her to, but she did it anyway."

"Why would she do that?" Moira demanded, glaring at me again.

I met her eyes. I had no idea where all this steel in my spine was coming from, but I was grateful for it. "She did it," I replied, "because she's kind." Then, unwisely, I added, "Something you know very little about."

The church ladies collectively gasped as if I'd set fire to a Bible.

For a moment, I thought Moira might attack me again. Instead, she said to Dormer, "You will lock him up until he tells you what he did with my Alexandra."

"Miss Moira," the deputy said patiently. "There's no evidence that Henry—"

"If you don't," she said with an icy calm. "I will telegraph the sheriff and demand that you be fired and replaced with someone who values law and order. And you know I can do it, Lucas Dormer."

To my considerable alarm, Dormer paled, his mouth working as if he'd bitten into something sour. Then he turned to the silent men around his desk, with Peter's mysterious plaster cast still atop it. "Gentlemen, why don't you leave this piece of evidence with me? I'll see if we can't get someone from Des Moines or maybe even Minneapolis to come give it a look. For now, though, I have some more pressing business."

With awkward nods, the salesman, the doctor, and the banker all excused themselves past Moira and the church ladies and departed. Of the three of them, only Peter spared me a regretful glance.

Then Dormer's hand closed over my bicep again and he said, "Got to put you back now, Henry."

"I want him to talk," Moira said dangerously. "I expect you to make him tell you what he did with my niece."

Offering no reply, the deputy escorted me back into my little cell, shut the door, and locked it with the key on his belt. He even met my eyes, careful to keep his back to the ladies, and offered me a pointed look that *seemed* to say he was on my side, and that we'd figure something out. It was a nice gesture.

I wished I believed it.

Chapter Four

I spent the whole day in that cell.

To be fair, Deputy Dormer treated me kindly. I didn't wait for meals or trips out to the privy, which was in the alley behind the building. He even chatted with me when he could, once Moira and her flock had gone, leaving us alone in his small office.

Time passed slowly.

Dormer spent much of the afternoon out searching for Alex and, hopefully, not telling everyone about the prime suspect he had locked up in his only cell. Not that I believed the good people of Van Meter would come by and lynch me. But I could guess just how far "innocent until proven guilty" would reach when dealing with a "no-good-beggar-and-drunk's-son."

With the sun slanted low through the windows that faced Main Street, the deputy finally returned. He looked exhausted and, when he saw me, his shoulders sagged even lower. Reading his face, I jumped up off the cot and met him at the bars.

"Nothing?" I asked.

"Nothing," he replied. "Where is she, Henry?"

"If I knew, I'd tell you."

"Would you?"

I nodded. "Whatever's going on, I can't help her in here. So, yeah. I'd tell you."

"By your own say-so, you're the one who saw her last."

"Believe me, I know it."

"Two nights ago," he said.

I nodded again. I hadn't told him about encountering Alex last night, partly because I wasn't sure I hadn't dreamed it. After all, it had only been from a distance and Alex hadn't said a word. She'd just come running, fanning the air in that weird way of hers. Given the near miss with Peter's shotgun, maybe my addled mind had simply conjured up the very thing I'd most wanted to see.

"God help you if she turns up dead," Dormer remarked.

"If she's dead, Mr. Dormer," I replied, meeting his eyes. "Then I'd be happy to join her."

He studied my face. "You love her." It wasn't a question or an accusation, merely a statement of fact.

"I do," I replied.

He shook his head, turned away, and left me to myself as the shadows in the small office grew longer.

I managed to sleep a little. But my dreams were filled with bright lights and loud shotgun blasts, which kept me away from anything like real rest. I suppose you could say I was waiting, though I had no conscious idea what *for*.

Well, the what-for came sometime after midnight. Dormer had departed until morning, having left me fresh water and a bit of cheese to see me through the night as well as making sure I'd done the necessary. He also left a bucket in the cell for emergencies, though I can fairly say that neither of us wanted me using it.

As things turned out, I didn't have to.

"Hank?"

I snapped roughly awake and sat bolt upright, staring into the near perfect darkness. For an instant, I felt certain I'd dreamed the voice.

But then it spoke again. "Hank?"

"Al?"

Footsteps approached, punctuated by the *tap, tap, tap* of a hickory cane. Then she was there, just a slender shadow beyond the bars, but definitely there, and despite everything my heart leapt at the sight of her. I felt a stupid grin spread across my face, which annoyed me.

"It's me," she said. She sounded sheepish.

"Al," I told her, climbing to my feet. "The next words out of your mouth had better be 'I'm sorry.'"

"I'm so sorry, Hank." She sounded like she meant it, and abruptly my anger at her blew away like the thin, fire-less smoke it was. That also annoyed me.

"Where have you *been*?" I demanded. "Your aunt figures I killed you! Either that, or I've got you locked up someplace!"

Her only reply was a kind of guilty moan.

So, I kept going. "Then she had me tossed in here until I tell her something she's willing to believe!"

"Well… I'm back now," Alex said, reaching one of her small pale hands through the bars. Almost without thinking, I stepped up and took it. Her skin felt warm and alive, and suddenly I wasn't annoyed at all. Whatever had been happening, wherever she'd been these last two days, she'd come for me — and that wasn't nothing.

"What time is it?" I asked. Then, blathering a bit, I added, "If you stay until morning, Dormer will see you're safe and sound and let me out. Then, we can — "

But she shook her head. "I can't stay."

"What? Why not?"

"I have to leave Van Meter, Hank."

The very idea turned my stomach to stone. "No!" I exclaimed. Still holding her hand as I was, I felt a nearly overwhelming desire to clamp down and pull her through the very bars, as if that were possible. The idea of going back to my life before Alex Harrer — well, "despair" just didn't describe it.

"I have to," she said, gently but firmly drawing her hand from mine. "But I couldn't go and leave you like this. So, I'm going to let you out."

"You're going to *what?*"

Alex held up a ring of keys that I recognized immediately. The last time I'd seen them, they'd been hanging from Deputy Dormer's belt.

"Where'd you — " I began. But she wordlessly and unerringly slipped the right key into the lock, turning the oiled bolt with a loud *clunk.*

"There," she said with a sigh.

I didn't move, not even when she opened the door and stood to one side expectedly, like a butler.

Moments passed, as moments do when nobody is doing or saying anything. Finally, looking more confused than upset, Alex asked, "What's wrong?"

I looked at the girl I loved and asked, "What am I to you?"

"What?"

"What am I to you?" I asked again, more forcefully this time.

Her beautiful face flashed with something. "Hank... I don't understand."

I didn't reply and didn't move, just waited.

Finally, she said, "You're my friend."

"You sure about that? Because I feel like maybe I'm more of a pet dog, one that you've got soft feelings toward because you've taught me all these cute tricks."

"What? No!" There was vehemence in her reaction, just enough to make me almost believe her.

"Then tell me the truth!" I exclaimed. "Tell me what's going on! Tell me what that monster is and what you have to do with it!"

More moments ticked by. I waited. At last, she replied in a small voice, "If I do, you won't believe me. Or worse, you *will* believe me, and you won't be my friend anymore."

"Alex," I said to her. "I'm locked up in here because your aunt figures I did something to you."

"I know..." she whispered. "That's why I came back, to let you out."

"And then what? Where am I going to go? I've never set foot outside Van Meter in my life. And, if Deputy Dormer comes back in the morning and finds me gone, every pair of eyes in the county will be looking for me. Is that what you want?"

"Of course not! But I..." Her words trailed off and, for the first time, I realized how tired she looked. No, more than just tired, completely and utterly spent.

Even so —

"You owe me the truth, Alexandra," I said.

"I know I do," she replied.

But before she could say another word, a sound split the air. It wasn't a scream or a cry or anything even remotely human. Instead, it was a gurgling crow, loud enough to make the hairs on the back of my neck stand straight up. But for all that, I recognized the noise. I'd heard it before.

As I watched, Alex spun around toward the street door — more, I thought, in alarm than surprise.

"What was that?" I demanded.

And my dream girl replied dismally, "*That* was my dog."

She ran for the door, her cane sweeping the space before her and I, my stubbornness and anger momentarily forgotten, followed right on her heels. We burst out together onto a darkened Main Street, with a light rain falling from a black sky. Understandably enough, given the hour, there was no one to be seen.

Alex hurried out into the middle of the street, her breath coming in hard gasps. "The light!" she cried. "Can you see her light?"

"Alex… what is it?"

"Hank, please!"

So, I let my eyes rake the surrounding rooftops, but saw only gloom and shadow.

Then, quite suddenly, a light appeared halfway down the block. It wasn't Visitor's light, however, but just an ordinary human glow in one of the windows above Fisher and White's Hardware and Furniture's darkened storefront. A moment later came the sound of a sash being thrown up, the noise faint but clear in the still night air.

"What is it?" Alex demanded, pulling on my arm. "What do you see?"

I tried to reply, but things happened too fast. A man's head filled the now open window. I recognized him at once. This was Otto White, "O.V." to pretty much everyone in town, the owner of the hardware and furniture store. I hadn't known he made his home above his shop, but it didn't surprise me. There was a lot of that in Van Meter.

What *did* surprise me was the revolver in Mr. White's hand. As I stared, with Alex still pulling on my arm, he leveled the weapon at a telephone pole on the same side of the street, not fifteen feet from his window.

For the first time, I spotted a shadow—a big one—perched atop the pole's crossbeam like a giant bird.

"Oh…" I heard myself say.

White fired.

The gunshot was deafening, the muzzle flash there and gone in an instant.

Beside me, Alex screamed.

Now, I didn't know O.V. White well. He'd never deigned to speak to the likes of me. But I had heard that he was a good shot, maybe even a marksman. So, I fully expected the creature atop the telephone pole to be struck and fall, or at least flinch. It did neither. Instead, the beast turned its horn toward the man, bathing him in what had to have been a blinding light. Mr. White gasped loudly and shielded his face with his hand, almost dropping the revolver in the process.

"What's happening?" Alex cried. She was sobbing now — and, instinctively, I draped one arm around her slight shoulders in a way that I never had before. But, at the same time, I couldn't take my eyes off the goings-on above the street.

Mr. White, the light still washing over him, suddenly covered his mouth and nose as if he'd smelled something so fierce that it gagged him. Then he sort of fell back through the window and disappeared from view.

"Is she all right?" Alex asked me through her sobs.

"I… think so," I replied. And it was true. The creature, seemingly unaffected by the gunshot, spread its huge wings and, for a moment, I thought it meant to take flight. But instead, it shook itself a little, maybe to throw off some of the rain, and then folded its wings again and began to descend the telephone poll.

"Hank!" Alexandra cried. "Tell me what's happening!"

"It's… eating the pole!"

Well, not really. But that was how it looked to me at the time. Years later, I'd watch a cinema news reel in which a parrot climbed down a tree by using its beak as a sort of a third claw. But standing there on that dark wet night as a sixteen-year-old boy who'd never seen a parrot, not even in pictures, "eating the pole" was the best I could do.

The creature leaned down and clamped its big beak around the stout wood and used it to leverage itself off the cross bean and down to where its claws could grip the pole. In this way, beak-claw-claw, it made its way down toward the street, not fast but steady.

As it did, I half-expected to see Mr. White reappear at his second-floor window, perhaps to fire down on the descending creature. Instead, *another* man appeared, this time from the opposite side of the same intersection. He came stumbling through the front door of one of the closed shops and, as with O.V. White, I recognized him at once.

Sid Gregg.

Sid was a man barely twenty and a decent sort. I liked him. But seeing him then just made my stomach lurch. He was staring at the telephone pole just as surely as I'd been, both of us little more than shadows in the night. If he'd noticed me, he gave no sign. Instead, all of his wide-eyed, slack-jawed attention seemed fixed on the creature that was still descending the pole.

Beak-claw-claw. Beak-claw-claw.

I felt Alex tug my arm again, more impatiently than before. "What's going on?"

"Sid's here," I replied.

"Sid? Sidney Gregg?"

Ahead of us, Visitor had reached the ground and now stood fully upright, roughly halfway between where Sid and I watched. Atop its head, that bright white light continued to pierce the curtain of rain, dashing to and fro as the creature looked around.

Alex all but screamed, "Where is she?"

"Just up ahead. Maybe... I don't know... twenty feet?"

With a cry, Alex ran forward, her cane tapping the road and her free hand waving frantically at the air.

All of a sudden, the creature's attention locked entirely on this slip of girl no more than a half its size. To my horror, it uttered another of those sheep-like bleats and started hopping toward her, jumping with both its feet, rather like a kangaroo. One hop. Then two. Then three.

"Alex!" I cried, making chase. "Get away from it!"

"It's okay! It's okay!" she called, though it wasn't until later that I understood she hadn't been talking to me.

"Hank! Is that you?" This came from behind the creature, further down the road. From Sid Gregg.

I wondered if I should risk answering him, but there simply wasn't time. The creature was right in front of Alex now, her blind face turned upward, its light, as bright as anything on any motorcar, pointing down at her, pinning her shadow to the street like it was a sunny noon instead of a rainy midnight.

And I was running. I was running full tilt, my feet slapping the muddy road, my hands reaching for my dream girl, determined to pull her away from that—

A train whistle, loud and plaintive, split the night.

I knew what it was at once. Any resident of Van Meter would. The "fast mail" was coming through town. It was a sound that I'd gotten so used to that I rarely noticed it, though I'd heard it could rattle the windows of the houses close to its tracks.

Alex recognized it too because she turned her face toward the sound with fresh alarm. At first, this confused me. Alex had lived in town for eight months and knew the mail train as well as anyone. But then I realized she wasn't alarmed for herself.

Looming over her, Visitor startled, its great body jerking. Then it crouched down, looking utterly alien, and launched itself forward.

By now, I'd reached Alexandra's back, and quickly took hold of her arm, intending to pull her out of the way of what I thought to be an imminent charge. Alex yelped at my touch, struggling wildly against me as the gigantic beast ran abreast of us.

With a cry, Alex pulled free of me so forcefully that I stumbled and nearly fell. Then, whirling around, she threw herself at the passing creature, her cane forgotten. Her leap was tremendous, more than I'd have imagined her capable, more than I'd have imagined *anyone* capable. For a moment, Alex Harrer seemed to float in the thing's wake. Then, before my stunned eyes, she somehow caught it, wrapping her arms around its neck and mounted it like a horse.

I screamed her name, only to watch helplessly as the rider and her unlikely mount continued down Main Street. Then, spreading its enormous, featherless wings, the creature took to the air, bearing Alex up with it.

For maybe half a minute, all I could do was watch, too shocked to really grasp what I was seeing.

Then, as Visitor and the girl soared ever higher, Sid Gregg came to stand beside me. Despite being a little older than me, he was a head shorter.

"Hank," he said. "What *is* that?"

I tried to answer, but no words would come.

Then he held up his right hand and I saw, with a numb sort of dismay, that he held a revolver in it. "Forgot I even had it," he said. "I'm so sorry! Maybe if I'd—"

"No," I told him, finally finding my tongue. "Mr. White shot at it, point blank, and it didn't seem to—"

Sid's eyes suddenly widened. "It's coming back!"

"What?"

He pointed. I looked.

The creature had cut a wide circle at the end of town and was now returning this way, still high but angled sharply downward, its wings spread but not beating the air, looking a bit like a huge kite. I couldn't tell if Alex was still riding it—"riding it," how hard it was to wrap my mind around such an idea.

"A second chance!" Sid Gregg exclaimed. He pushed me clear and brandished his pistol in both hands as the thing that had been haunting

Van Meter leveled off just a few feet above the muddy, rain-soaked road.

And yes. I could now clearly see the girl still astride it.

"No!" I exclaimed. "You might hit Alex!"

"I'm a good shot," Sid promised me. "I'll wait'll it's close."

That seemed a stupid plan in the extreme. But, before I could protest further, the creature bore down on us. As it did, I could just make out Alex waving her hand frantically in our direction.

Sidney Gregg yelled, "Bang!"

I blinked, my mind turning to mud as it had last night in front of the bank.

Then they were upon us, beast and rider, little more than a pale blur. I had a scant instant to register Alex's desperate look as she reached for me in passing. Her small hand caught the front of my shirt and pulled me off my feet with astounding strength. In the next instant, I was airborne, flipping over the creature's back. I landed awkwardly, and hard enough to knock the wind from my lungs. I gasped and scrambled for purchase along its smooth hide before Alex managed to get hold of my hands and yank them around her own waist.

"Hold on!" she told me.

Hold on I did as Visitor carried us up and away into the night, with poor Sid till yelling "bang" with ever-increasing urgency.

I admit it. I screamed.

I screamed a lot.

I had no idea what Alex was holding onto. It wasn't as if this beast wore a saddle or bridle. Its skin was smooth and slick from rain, and it bobbed through the night sky like a small boat on a stormy sea, listing with the air currents. More than once I felt sure I would vomit and only avoided it by squeezing my eyes shut—

—and, of course, screaming.

Yet, for all that, I could tell where were headed.

The old coal mine.

It had closed back in '02 after some kind of strike—I didn't know the details—and had been abandoned ever since. The nearby Platt Brick Company was still up and running though, and they still owned the land that the mine occupied. In its day it had been a serious coal mine, the deepest in the country. Because of that, nobody was allowed near the site. The last thing Dormer wanted was for some curious kid to be killed exploring the old place.

Both the mine and the brick factory were located on cleared land outside of town, close to the train tracks. As we overflew those tracks, I risked a nervous peek, and immediately understood two things. The first was that Visitor was spiraling us downward toward the mine's main entrance, a vertical shaft easily thirty feet in diameter and only accessible via a massive bore hole.

The second was that peeking had been a very bad idea.

This time I *did* vomit, the spew getting whisked away in the creature's slipstream. Even so, I heard Alex, to whom I still clung as if she were a life preserver, groan in disgust.

"Sorry," I muttered.

She didn't reply.

It was still raining as Visitor landed in the mud only steps from the bore hole. Since its closure, heavy boards had been fastened over it to deter trespass. But I saw now that these had been either pulled or pushed free, and not with tools. No, something more akin to brute force had torn through here, the kind of brute force that an eight-foot-tall, winged creature might be able to muster.

"You can let go of me now, Hank," Alex said.

And I tried. But my arms didn't seem to want to unlock. It didn't help that my blood rushed loudly behind my ears and my stomach was in my throat.

"Hank," she said patiently. "It's okay. You're safe."

"You're safe," not *"we're safe."*

For some reason, that simple difference reignited my anger.

I released her and tried to climb off the creature, which had knelt down helpfully, almost as if trained for just this sort of thing. Even so, my body shook with nerves and I slipped at the last minute, landing on my back in the mud. That, by itself, would have been embarrassing but not disastrous, except for the broken brick *under the* mud that caught me squarely at the base of my skull.

I instantly saw stars.

"Hank?" Alex called, sounding alarmed. I heard rather than saw her drop down beside him and kneel to touch my head. Fresh pain shot out from the point of contact, and despite the rain, I could feel warm blood running down the back of my neck. "Oh no…" my dream girl muttered. "No. No. No."

"I'm okay," I told her. Then, much to her dismay, I tried to rise. Instantly, the world spun, and I flopped back again, this time on my buttocks.

When I looked over at Alex, she was flapping her hand in the way she had before. I stared at her and, reading her deep concern, tried to reiterate that I was fine.

Instead, the world around me went dark, just like all the times before.

Am I ever again going to get a normal night's sleep?

At the last moment, a face filled my line of sight, a huge, sloping head with a shining white light above its dark eyes. For an instant, I thought the creature meant to eat me. Instead, snuffling my face in an odd but not aggressive way, it suddenly produced a tongue as long as my forearm—and licked me with it.

"Ugh," I heard myself mutter.

And then I was gone.

CHAPTER FIVE

I awoke in perfect darkness, the kind that makes you wonder if you're really awake or trapped in some nightmare. For a moment, I stared blindly. Then I tried to sit up, but something pinned the back of my head to the floor, something sticky.

So, I screamed — again.

"Hank! Stay calm!"

It was Alex's voice, coming at me out of the blackness. "I can't see," I exclaimed. Then, in an even higher pitch: "Something's got my head!"

"Oh! I'm sorry. Hold on..."

Sudden white light pierced my eyes like pokers, making me gasp and cover my face with one hand. With the other, I felt beneath my head and found a substance there, cold, and thicker than mud.

"Leave it alone, Hank!"

I blinked, my eyes adjusting to the glare. Alex hovered over me, looking wet and disheveled but beautiful anyhow. She wore the same frock she'd had on when we'd encountered the creature last night, or earlier *this* night, or —

What time was it, anyway?

Then, as I looked around, more pressing concerns presented themselves. We were in an uneven, rocky chamber perhaps a dozen feet to a side. And standing against one wall, its wings tucked in close to its body, Visitor regarded me passively. It was its weird horn light that filled the surrounding space.

Just a dog... I thought.

A dog you can ride like an ugly Pegasus.

Meeting Alex's sightless eyes, I asked, "What am I lying on?"

"A poultice," she replied. "To help with the swelling."

"Like what you got me for poison ivy?"

"Much stronger. It's made from lichen that grows in the deep places." She swallowed in a way that looked almost painful. "I'm so sorry you got hurt. It's all my fault."

There was truth to that, though I didn't say so. Besides, whatever this stuff was, it seemed to be working. My head didn't hurt at all. Come to think of it, even my arm had stopped stinging. So, I raised that and, sure enough, Dr. Alcott's bandage had been replaced with a thin layer of sticky poultice.

Good stuff.

Putting that aside, I said, "Answers, Al. It's time."

"I know."

"Start with the funny looking dog," I said, nodding toward the creature.

Alex actually laughed at that, but it didn't last. "I know how strange she must look to you. But I raised her from a hatchling and it's how I think of her."

"Her?"

"She's a girl."

"Sure," I said. "But what *is* it… she?"

"That's… hard to explain."

I waited.

She seemed to struggle for words, her expression pained and helpless.

I waited some more.

Finally, she said, "They don't have a name, at least not in English. Or any other language you might have heard of."

I blinked. "How's that?"

"She comes from a place far below ground, a place without light and where sound… well, sound doesn't work reliably."

"Okayyyy," I said, drawing out the word. I wish I could say I figured Alex was crazy, or maybe she'd hit her head too. But I didn't believe either of those things. No, my belly wasn't twisting into knots because I thought she was lying or deluded. It was doing so because I knew she *wasn't*.

"And she's your… pet?"

Alexandra nodded, wearing an expression that made me think she expected me to protest, maybe exclaim something like, "Monsters can't be pets!"

But I was kind of past that now. So, instead, I said, "Since she's got no name in English, mind if I give her one? I came up with it last night, while I was petting her on the street just before you showed up."

"What name?" she asked in a small voice.

"How about… Visitor?"

I was rewarded with a tearful smile.

Then, I said, "I'm sorry about the people in town, the ones who shot at her. They were scared."

"I know."

"Except they didn't *all* shoot. Dr. Alcott and Sid wanted to, but they didn't."

She stiffened. I got the sense she'd expected this line of inquiry but hadn't been looking forward to it. "They *tried* to," she told me. "But I stopped them."

"How?"

"You won't believe me."

I glanced at the huge, winged beast who stood stoically at the rear of the chamber, filling the space with its unearthly light. "You'd be surprised what I'm ready to believe."

Alex sat back on her heels; her expression thoughtful. I got the feeling she was weighing her options and it troubled me that only one of those "options" involved telling me the truth. Finally, she shook her head miserably. "I don't know where to start."

"The beginning's usually a good place."

"The beginning?"

"Ain't that where the best stories always start?"

"Isn't," she corrected, pretty much automatically, I thought.

I didn't reply.

Instead, I waited some more.

Alex Harrer took a long deep breath, like the kind you draw in right before diving into a cold lake. Then she said, "My people are older than yours. Much older. But, unlike you, we didn't evolve on this world. We come from… someplace else."

I tried to process this, lying there with my head and arm covered in poultice.

Finally, though it took some looking, I found my tongue. "That's not true."

"Yes, Hank. It is."

"You're a girl."

"Yes. But not a human girl."

"That's crazy, Al."

"I know it must seem that way to you."

"I'm *looking* at you," I said, and there was so much behind that statement that it caught in my throat.

"But you're not *seeing* me," she replied. "You're only seeing what I... *allow* you to see."

I tried to translate this into something resembling sense but couldn't. The more Alex talked, the less real it all seemed. Finally, painfully, I said the only thing I could think of. "I don't believe you."

"Told you so."

That annoyed me. It always annoyed me when we quarreled and she was proven right, which truthfully was most of the time. "All right. Let's pretend I *do* believe you. Let's pretend that you're a girl from another world who can make people see things and do things. What is that? Magic? Space magic maybe?"

"Olfactory manipulation," she said.

"And what's that called when it's at home?"

She almost smiled at that.. "Humans don't have a name for it yet. You don't even know it exists. But your sense of smell is much more than you think it is. More than any of your other senses, your olfactory receptors are closely tied to the way you perceive the world."

I stared at her for several seconds. "Al, I don't have the foggiest notion of what you're saying."

She sighed, seemed to steady herself, and then tried again. "My people live beneath the surface, in places of absolute darkness, much darker than this chamber, where sound reverberates and can't be trusted. So, over millions of years, we've evolved a language based entirely on scent."

"Smells."

She nodded.

"So, you talk to each other by... what? Farting?" I was being flippant, and I knew it. But this was all so utterly ridiculous. Then I glanced over at Alex's "dog" and found myself wondering how true that was.

Alex scowled. "Don't be crass. We're able to selectively emit specific odors that can convey anything from our names to complex concepts and ideas. It's a much subtler and far much comprehensive language than anything you hairless apes can manage with your lips and tongues."

Now *that* sounded like an insult.

"So, Alex Harrer isn't your real name?" I asked crossly.

"No."

"And your real name is... what? A smell?"

"Yes," she said, glaring at me insofar as a blind girl can glare at anyone.

"Alex, that's crazy."

"No, Hank Trotter, it isn't. It's just a bit outside your imagination."

It was a tone I knew well. Half-condescension and half-insult. In the time I'd known her, Alex had only ever employed that old chestnut when she thought I wasn't living up to what she considered to be my intellectual potential. When I wasn't "thinking."

So now I *thought*.

And the more I thought, the crazier it all seemed. Except—

—except that it also explained some things. Like sudden blackouts. Like sane men shouting "bang" instead of firing their guns. Like a blind girl's uncanny way of coming and going without the benefit of eyes.

"Smelling is what you do instead of seeing," I said carefully, as if testing the words.

"It's a little more complicated than that. But yes."

"And you can do things to people... using smells." I struggled to remember the term. "Olfactory manipulation."

This time, her "yes" was more sheepish.

"Dr. Alcott and Sid... they both tried to shoot at poor Visitor. But instead, they just said "bang," like kids playing with toy guns. That was you, wasn't it?"

"Yes."

"They *think* they fired because you *made* them think that."

"Yes."

"By... flapping your hand at them."

She nodded. "I had to transmit my olfactory message quickly. I was afraid they'd hurt her. Her skin is thick, very thick. But enough bullets could—"

"And me? You used it on me?"

"I... had to."

"You put me to sleep, didn't you? Snuffed me out like a candle flame."

A tear rolled down her cheek. "I had to find her, keep her safe, and I knew I couldn't do that with you tagging along."

"Tagging along. Like a puppy. That's what I am to you, ain't it?"

"No! You're my friend!"

The vehemence in her voice pleased me, I won't deny. But I still wasn't sure if I believed her.

"Show me what you really look like," I said.

The request took her by surprise, though it shouldn't have. Hadn't she already told me she wasn't human? After a few moments, she shook her head and declared, "No."

"You owe me that," I said.

"No."

"You do, damn it!"

"Language, Hank," she admonished, a reflex.

"Just shut up! You ain't my teacher anymore! You've been lying to me since the day we met!"

Her face twisted into such an anguished expression that it very nearly drowned my anger yet again. But this time, I wasn't going to let it.

"Hank—" she began.

But I ran right over her, sitting up so suddenly that the sticky poultice popped free with a weird sucking sound. As I did, she hopped back on her hunches in surprise, and maybe a little alarm. Nearby, Visitor uttered a nervous bleat. The poultice immediately started sliding down the back of my neck, but I didn't care. "You been using your smells on me. You're doing it now, keeping me from what seeing what you really are!"

"I… do that to everyone. I have to." And then she said something that stopped my anger in its tracks, something that changed, if not everything, then certainly a lot.

She said, "I'm the first to come up here."

"Well, not the first, exactly. But I've been here longer than any of my people who have visited the surface. I'm the first to have really lived among you as a human. You see, my people arrived in Earth's early days, long before life evolved. Back then, the air wasn't at all the way it is now, making it impossible to survive on the surface. So, we went deep below the planet's crust and made our home in the vast empty caverns we found there."

I listened to this feeling a hundred things, from scared to fascinated to almost physically ill. She still looked like Alex—my Alex—but at the same time not. This girl seemed older, wiser, and much more distant. Now I hadn't spent a lot of time in a classroom. But I recalled the schoolmaster's manner being much the same.

I was being lectured at.

"Millions of years passed," she said. "Not the five thousand or so that Pastor Robinson espouses, but millennia upon millennia. And, in all that time, we lived in peace and contentment in the deep places. We built cities. Raised crops. We multiplied. Now, we're not a naturally adventurous race. We came to this world from one that was dying, out of desperation rather than exploration. So, for most of our history, we've had little interest in what was going on up here. But some centuries ago, a few of us got curious. And what we found stunned us. The violent world we'd first colonized had matured and flourished. What's more, it had brought forth intelligent life! Primitive, mind you, but intelligent."

"Primitive?"

"Sorry, Hank. But yes."

I didn't say anything, though I gave her a look that conveyed what I thought of her evaluation of humans. Then I remembered she was blind and suddenly worried she might be overestimating our "intelligence."

Alex explained, "My people don't know war. We don't know crime. We live in peace and have since before the first native lifeforms existed on this world."

"Bully for you," I remarked sourly.

"I'm giving you what you wanted, Hank. Answers."

"By telling me you're better than I am."

"No!" And her vehemence surprised me. "Not better. Different. Older. Wiser. That's all."

"Does that include you?" I asked.

"Me?"

"You say this isn't what you really look like, and you won't show me what you *do* look like. Fine. But are you really a sixteen-year-old girl? Or are you different, older, and wiser but not better than me?"

"I'm..." she began, fumbling. "I'm... young. A child, like you. In fact, I'm too young to be out in the human world, if that helps you understand."

"Then why are you here?"

"I... ran away."

"From home?"

She nodded.

"Why?"

"Because I wanted to experience the surface world! I wanted to feel the sun on my face, wanted to learn this weird verbal language of yours. I wanted to know what it's like to have the wind touch my skin. So, eight months ago, I snuck away from my family, my friends, my people, and came up through one of the lesser-used routes."

"The old mine," I said.

She nodded again.

"Is that where we are now? In the mine?"

"Yes. Close to where I came up. Usually, my people visit after careful preparation and stay for only a few days. But I arrived without any sort of pre-arranged backstory. Just *me*."

"Then how did you end up as Moira Van Meter's niece?"

"Luck, mostly. The first people I came across worked at the brick factory. Instinctively, I made them see this face, hoping I would seem harmless. I'd heard that humans could be violent if confronted with something even a little bit outside their experience."

I almost argued. But then I remembered the townsfolks' guns and closed my mouth again.

Maybe, just maybe, Alex had a point.

She said, "They saw a waif, lost and confused, and took me to Deputy Dormer's office. On the way, I asked some careful questions about the town and learned the name of its wealthiest resident. A spinster aunt seemed like as good a place as any to stay, at least in the short term. So, when I met with the deputy, I told him I was Moira's great niece, recently orphaned. Then he took me to see Moira, who welcomed me into her home."

"Just like that? Nobody questioned you?"

"I didn't let them."

"You didn't—" Then I stopped, remembering. "That olfactory manipulation."

She nodded, having enough decency to look embarrassed about it.

I said, "You can make us see what you want us to see."

"Yes."

"Hear what you want us to hear."

"Yes."

"*Think* what you want us to think."

"That's... harder."

"You said you planned to stay with Ms. Moira only for the 'short term.' What did that mean?"

"Van Meter's a small place," she replied. "I wanted to experience your world, visit cities, smell the ocean, the dessert, things that don't exist where I come from."

"Then why didn't you?"

To my surprise, she took my hand in both of hers. Immediately, I lost myself in the feel of her warm, soft skin against mine. I reminded myself that it was an illusion, that she'd been manipulating my mind since the day we'd met—that she was, in fact, doing it right now. But she was so close to me, and despite everything, she remained my dream girl.

"*You*, Hank," she said. "I stayed because of you."

"Me?" I tried to say more, but the words wouldn't come.

"Of course. From my second day in Van Meter, when I saw you sitting outside Mr. Dunn's bank, I knew immediately you were special."

"I'm a beggar," I protested.

"Begging is something you do," she told me. "Not something you *are*. What you *are* is kind, intelligent, and... well... pure."

"Pure?" I exclaimed. "Al, I stink worse than a cart full of horse dung. Ask my pop. Heck, ask anybody!"

I expected to her laugh. She didn't. Instead, she brought her face so close to mine that I could feel her warm breath on my skin. "Henry Trotter, I love the way you smell. I always have. But it's your heart I'm talking about. That's what's pure."

"Then why didn't you tell me the truth?"

"Because I'd have lost you!" Then, to my no small shock, she started crying.

So, I did something I'd never done before. I pulled her into my arms. This proved rather sticky, given the poultice. But she didn't seem to mind. Her head settled on my shoulder; her small hands nestled against my chest.

I didn't say, "I love you."

I wanted to, but I was just too scared.

Nearby, Visitor uttered a plaintive bleat. I didn't know if our embrace pleased her, frightened her, or if she was simply bored of standing there lighting our conversation with her glowing horn. But, in any case, when she bleated again, Alex raised her head and turned toward the creature. She said nothing, but Visitor went silent anyway, shuffling from three-toed foot to three-toed foot, looking almost like a frustrated toddler.

"Is that really your dog?" I asked Alex.

"She's my pet, my friend."

"What's the horn light for?"

"Her kind are descended from creatures who used to inhabit this world. Dinosaurs, you call them. Nobody remembers when or how, but we domesticated them. They're not blind like we are, but their vision is complex and sensitive. Her horn light helps her see in the deep places. They don't do anything for us, of course, so we tend to ignore them."

"And her wings? What're they for?"

"For flying, of course!"

"How much flying can you do in caves?"

"Image caverns that are a hundred miles across and half that high," she said. "With floors that are often uneven and frequently flooded. My people make our homes in structures that we build high along the walls of these places. The only way to get to them is by air."

"So, you ride visitors."

"Yes."

I tried to picture what Alex was describing. The closest I could come was an old photograph of ancient cliff dwellings in New Mexico. But those folks hadn't ridden dinosaurs.

"What did she do to Mr. White after he shot at her."

"Oh. That was a defensive mechanism. If threatened, her kind can release a scent that… confounds whoever's threatening them."

"Like a skunk."

"Well, no. I mean, you can't smell it consciously. But it'll still work on you."

"Smells you can't smell," I mused. "That's quite a 'pet' you've got there."

Alex explained, "I've known her all my life. Growing up, we were inseparable. The hardest thing about coming here wasn't leaving my family so much as leaving *her*."

Visitor bleated again, more softly this time. Then she hopped forward and lowered her huge head so that Alex could reach up and stroke it.

A girl and her dog, I thought.

Alex said, "But, hard as it was for both of us, being separated like this for so long, I never imagined that she'd come looking for me."

"So that's what's been going on all week? Visitor's been looking for you?"

She nodded. "Ordinarily, down in our cities, we find each by our signature scent. It's easy. I imagine it's a bit like spotting someone you know from some distance away and going toward them. But up here, with so many strange smells… well, they confuse everything. I didn't get a whiff of her until after dark that first night. I came back to this mine, but she wasn't here."

"So, you came to me," I said.

"Yes. I guessed that she'd be searching for where my signature scent was strongest, and that would likely take her either to Moira's house or downtown. Turned out to be downtown. The problem is she's nervous, completely out of her element. That first night, Mr. Griffith's motor car frightened her. With each passing night, she's been getting bolder. But, as a result, she keeps being shot at, scared off. Until last night, I was never able to get close enough for her to recognize me."

"So where have you been these past two days?"

"I assumed she'd found a cave to hide in during the day. Daylight's too much for her. So, I've been searching. But… it's hard."

"Sure, it's hard!" I exclaimed. "You're blind!"

She didn't reply.

I shook my head. "You should have told me, Al. At least some of it. Instead, you *manipulated* me. Three straight nights you've put me to sleep. Granted, this last time, I did *this* to myself." I fingered the lump on the back of my head, under the muck, only to find it almost completely gone. Apparently, Alex's poultice worked marvels. "You could have straight up asked for my help."

"Would you have given it?"

"Of course!"

"Even now that you know I'm not… human?"

I looked at her, feeling a little sick to my stomach.

Finally, I said, "I'm sorry."

She sat up, looking genuinely perplexed. "What for?"

"That you think so little of me. But I guess I understand. I'm not smart… at least not smart enough for all this."

"Hank, you're brilliant," she said. "You're going to be a great writer someday."

"Because of you."

"No, because of *you*. All I've done is teach you some English."

"You didn't always know English?"

"Of course not. Before I left home, I'd never heard a spoken language in my life. But it's actually pretty simple and I picked up quickly."

"How quickly?" I asked, thinking of the brickmen who'd found her.

She shrugged. "Minutes. Once I had the syntax, it was easy enough to replicate the sounds."

Older, I thought, a bit dismally. *Wiser.*

Better.

She said, "But it wasn't until I was settled in Aunt Moira's house, and she started giving me books to read that I learned about the written word."

"Books?" I asked, confused.

"Braille."

"Oh. They use dots for letters, right?"

"Yes. It took me an hour or so to get a feel for it. But once I did, I read everything my aunt provided for me."

"An hour," I muttered. "Just how smart are you?"

"Smart enough to know a good man when I find one," she said, which struck me as the kindest compliment I'd ever been paid. Then, before I could reply, she climbed to her feet and offered me one small hand. "Come on and meet her. Properly, I mean."

"What?"

She nodded toward Visitor. "Come and say hello."

Tentatively, I put my hand in hers. A moment later, I was on my feet. My dream girl, it appeared, was stronger than she looked. I wobbled on legs that seemed to have forgotten what they were for. Alex apparently sensed this, or smelled it, because she supported me with a hand on my elbow.

"I'm okay," I insisted.

Maybe a little reluctantly, she let me go.

For a moment, I just stood there facing her with my back to the creature. But before I could turn around, Visitor abruptly shoved her massive, elongated head under my arm. At first, I started. But then she let out a little bleat, one that sounded timid and harmless. So, a bit to my chagrin, I found myself hugging her one-handedly.

"They're gentle creatures," Alex told me. "It would never occur to her to hurt anyone."

"And yet all humans have done is shoot at her," I muttered.

Alex didn't reply.

"Okay," I said, stroking Visitor's long curved cheek. "What happens now?"

"Now, I take her home."

That stopped me cold. "You're leaving?"

"Hank, I have to. If she stays here, she'll be killed. She has a very thick hide, but she's not made of lead. You're right. All anyone does is shoot at her and, sooner rather than later, one of those shots is going to pierce her skin. I can't risk that. I *have* to see her safely back."

"Oh," I muttered.

Inside, however, my guts had turned to ice.

"I *have* to take her home," Alex said again. "But, to do that, I need your help… one last time."

She led me, *us*, out of the cavern and deeper into the mine. There's no expressing just how vast the network of tunnels and pits were in this dark place. A person could easily get lost, which was why the town had closed it after the coalmen left. Yet Alex navigated it with apparent ease, not even needing her hickory cane. I asked her how that was, if she were truly as blind as she appeared to be. Her answer, however, didn't exactly satisfy me. "Your world has much fewer walls than mine. I need my cane because it's so very *big* out there. But down here, well down here, eyes aren't the only… or best… way to see."

Visitor kept pace behind us, her horn light casting our shadows across the uneven floor. Being so large, she kept her wings tucked in close and stayed mostly on all fours, making her look more like a long-headed lizard than any sort of flying beast. More than once, when Alex paused to get her bearings, Visitor brought her huge head under my arm again.

I understood. She was nervous and wanted some physical contact. *Like any dog.*

"Here," Alex finally said. "This is where we came up, first me, then her eight months later."

It was a vertical shaft, perhaps ten feet in diameter. But how deep it was, I couldn't tell, as it had been flooded. Black water filled it to barely a foot below the lip.

"That ain't good," I remarked.

I expected her to correct my grammar. She didn't.

"No," she agreed instead. "I'm not sure when it happened. I found it this way when I came looking for Visitor a couple of days ago. She wasn't here at the time, but *this* was."

"I guess you can't swim?"

"I can," Alex replied. "We both can. But the shaft is two hundred feet deep, all flooded. Worse, the entire level below is underwater. We'd never make it. Not even close."

"So… you're stuck here?" I asked, unable to keep the hope out of my voice.

"Maybe not." And with that, she started along a tributary tunnel, one that lead sharply downward. After a moment, I followed, with Visitor close behind me.

We walked for ten more minutes before we came to a second shaft, much bigger than the first and apparently dry. "Where's this one go?" I asked.

"Only about a hundred feet down," Alex replied. "It's a longer route, and much more convoluted. But it'll get us there."

My heart sank. "Then what do you need me for?"

She pointed down into the shaft. I looked, but the darkness was like a wall. So, on a command mostly *smelled*, Visitor pushed past me and shone her horn light deep into the gloom.

Instantly, the problem became evident. Sometime ago, the shaft had collapsed. Rocky debris now filled it, end to end, starting maybe a dozen feet down.

Completely impassable.

"There's no way to move the water in the other shaft," Alex explained. "But I think… I *hope*…there's something we can do about this."

"Like what?" I asked. Then I understood. "You're talking about dynamite."

She nodded.

I gave myself a moment to consider things. Here stood my dream girl. I'd loved her since the day we'd met, though I'd always been too afraid, or too intimidated, to say so. She was my Al, my sometimes teacher and my only friend, the sole person in my life who'd ever believed that I could be more than just a street beggar. Even now, with her blonde hair tangled and filthy and her alabaster skin layered in grime, her beauty struck me almost like a physical blow.

Except it's all a lie.

A smell.

"You brought me here," I said, "because you think I can get you dynamite."

I expected her to deny it. Instead, she replied, "Partly," the word punctuated by another single tear. Was the tear part of the disguise, the smell, or was it the genuine sentiment of a desperate girl reaching out to her friend for help?

How could I possibly know?

I said, "If I get it for you, you'll use it to blow open this tunnel. Then you and Visitor will go home."

"Yes."

"And never come back?"

"No, Hank." Was there sorrow in her words? I wasn't sure.

"And if I *don't* get the dynamite?"

"Then *they'll* come."

"Who?"

"The men in town. They'll come for Visitor… and they'll kill her."

I looked again at the creature, no longer any sort of monster, that still lit our conversation with its unearthly — or, perhaps more aptly, "underearthly" — light. "They won't come here at all," I told Alex. "No one has for years. If she stays here and stops showing up in town every night, she'll be fine."

Alex replied, "She *can't* stay here, Hank. For one, there's no food. For another, she's a flying creature. She *needs* the space to spread her wings. Without that, she'll die… slowly, maybe, but she'll definitely die."

I almost made another suggestion. I almost asked her to run away with me, all three of us. We could go somewhere remote, where Visitor could fly all she wanted and no one would ever see her, where Alex wouldn't be the niece of Van Meter's First Citizen and I wouldn't be a beggar. There had to be places like that in a world this big.

Didn't there?

But then I remembered I wasn't looking at a human girl, not really. And I knew, without asking, what her answer would be.

Alex Harrer was going home, and I was going to be alone again. That was the truth of it. All I had to do now was accept that truth, painful as it was, and help her, because that's what friends do.

"How much dynamite do you need?" I asked.

Chapter Six

Alex led us past the original chamber and through an archway that opened into an upwardly sloping tunnel. Visitor followed along, her big head tucked awkwardly under my arm for almost the entire way, her horn-light illuminating our path.

Eventually, we came to the bottom of a huge shaft, one that reached up to an opening high overhead, through which I could see the night sky. Rickety-looking wooden steps led upward, fastened to the shaft walls and winding around them as they ascended.

"Up there's the mine entrance," Alex reported needlessly.

"I know," I said. "I can—"

Visitor let out a gurgling crow so loud it made my ears hurt. As her head was still tucked affectionately under my arm, I jumped at least a foot, and almost fell over when she pulled away from me and straightened to her full height.

"Somebody's up there!" Alex said in a sharp whisper.

"Who?" I couldn't see or hear anyone. We had to be a hundred feet down.

"I think it's Mr. Platt," she replied.

"How can you tell?"

"It smells like him."

"Sure," I said. "Where is he?"

"I think he's right at the edge of the bore hole. He *must* have heard Visitor just now."

That wasn't good news. Nothing on Earth made a sound like Alex's gentle, enormous pet when she was alarmed. And given everything else that had been happening in Van Meter all week—

"Let me go talk to him," I suggested. "Maybe I can—"

But she cut me off. "You busted out of jail, remember? Half the town's probably looking for you."

It was a bitterly valid point. But it also raised a question. "How long have we been down here?"

"You were unconscious for most of the day. The poultice I gave you worked but it took some time. It's now the middle of the night on Saturday. Sorry. I should have told you that."

So, I'd been missing for a whole day. Alex was right. Dormer would have recruited every able-bodied man for a search party. Moira Van Meter would have insisted on it. I didn't know J.L. Platt well, but he was respected in town. His family had owned and managed the mine for at least two generations and, now that the mine was closed, Platt ran the nearby brick plant, which employed plenty of folks in Van Meter. All of that meant two things. First, if he reported back about hearing Visitor's loud crow, Dormer was bound to take the claim seriously. And second, if I went up there now, I'd be back in that cell inside of an hour, middle-of-the-night or no middle-of-the-night.

"What do we do?" I asked Alex.

"I… don't know…"

Behind us, perhaps picking up on her mistress' fear, Visitor crowed again, as loud as before. Alex tried to calm her, but her pet was having none of it. As I stepped aside and watched, Alex and Visitor held each other, the sight alien and yet weirdly natural.

A girl and her dog, indeed.

"Can you… maybe… hide her?" I asked, a little desperately.

Alex looked at me, not comprehending.

"Can you use your smell stuff to make her invisible? Or make her look like a simple cow or something?"

She shook her head. "I can change what *I* look like. I might even be able to change what *you* look like, though that would be harder. But Visitor's too big. It wouldn't work on her."

I nodded and looked down at my shoes, thinking furiously. Now I'd never been what anyone would call a strategist. But with Alexandra and her pet in so much trouble, I suppose one could say I rose to the occasion.

"You can change what you look like?" I asked her.

Alexandra, who'd gone back to hugging the still crowing creature, replied, "Yes."

I said, "Then I've got an idea."

What followed was the uncanniest experience of my life — up until that point, anyway. Once I made my plan clear to Alex, I was pleased to see her despair recede a bit, replaced by a stalwart practicality as she pointed out weak spots and suggested improvements. Together, it took us perhaps ten minutes to sort everything out, during which time Visitor's anxious crows, still too loud, at least became less frequent.

Finally, Alex asked me, "Are you sure about this?"

I nodded, though I wasn't, not at all.

"Okay, then," she proclaimed with a sigh. "Hank, I'm sorry for all the trouble."

I nodded because, well, what else *could* I do?

And, before my eyes, Al changed. In place of her waif-like frame wrapped in a grimy frock, there stood a miniature version of Visitor. It was perhaps five feet tall, with a wingspan at least that wide. The head was long and slightly curved and, in the center of its forehead was a horn, identical to, though smaller than, Visitor's own.

I gasped and put a hand to my mouth. Even though I'd known what was coming and Alex had assured me that it was simply another "olfactory manipulation," and definitely *not* what she actually looked like, the metamorphosis shook me to my core.

Then this new creature spoke. "It's still me, Hank."

I tried to nod but couldn't quite manage it. My knees turned weak, in no small part because I'd recognized Alex's voice without the miniature Visitor's long mouth moving at all. It was as if she'd spoken directly into my mind.

That made me suddenly wonder if she always had.

With some effort, I managed to find my tongue. "I'll... I'll meet you where we said." Then, because it seemed a good idea, I added, "Be careful."

"You, too," she told me. "Stand back."

I stood back.

Moments later, Alex and Visitor — that is, the big Visitor and the little Visitor, spread their leathery wings and took to the air. As I watched, transfixed, the two of them exploded out into the night sky. In reality, Alex was riding on Visitor as she had before. Her wings and her independent flying were just part of the illusion.

Nevertheless, it was beautiful

Moments later, I heard a man, presumably Mr. Pratt, cry out in alarm and issue more than one expletive. Then, as the loud flapping of wings receded into the distance, I kept listening. Only silence followed. Presumably, the decoy had worked, and Mr. Pratt was off to raise the alarm.

I started climbing the stairs, hurrying toward the surface the old-fashioned way, without wings.

It was time to do my part.

I emerged from the mine into a dark, overcast night. As fresh air filled my lungs, I looked hurriedly around and saw that I was alone.

I took it as a good omen.

As I made my way to the tree line, however, heading in the general direction of town, I spotted lanterns perhaps a quarter mile away. They came from the brick factory, where a group of men had gathered. Despite the dark and distance, I thought I could see Mr. Pratt among them, talking animatedly. Mostly likely he was telling his story to his employees and had already sent someone on horseback to notify Dormer that Pratt had found the "monster's" lair. Before long, a lot more men would converge here, reasoning, as Alex and I hoped, that the two creatures witnessed just now flying away from the mine would return there before morning.

I had to have what I needed by then.

Dreading every step, I ran as fast as I could to the last place I wanted to go.

Home.

The shack stood dark and still in its field. I approached as quietly as haste would allow, keeping low as I neared the only window, since I knew that on some nights he stayed up late, just looking out at nothing.

But there was no face there, the glass dark.

I reached the door and gently tested the old latch. It slipped easily, letting me into the small space that had been my childhood prison. Not so much as a candle was lit, which made sense I supposed, given the hour.

I listened. Usually, he snored loudly, but now there was nothing but my own haggard breathing. As my eyes adjusted to the gloom, however, I spotted him on his cot, curled up under a threadbare blanket, his head resting on a straw pillow.

It looked — wrong.

Despite myself, I whispered, "Pop?" Even in his deepest drunk, he should have stirred a little at that. But there was nothing. I took a step toward the cot, then another, a fresh sense of unreality dropping over me, stunting my emotions.

Standing over him, it struck me how *small* he seemed.

My heart pounded as I knelt down and, with a trembling hand, touched the skin of his cheek.

It was cold and hard.

"Oh, Pop…" I muttered. "What did you do?"

That was when I saw the brown bottle clamped in one of his hands, his fingers so stiff around it that I didn't think I could have pried it loose if I'd wanted to. Instead, I leaned over, careful not to touch him further, and sniffed what wafted out from its open neck.

No smell. None at all.

Grain alcohol.

Either the old man had been so desperate for liquor and, without me providing him with money from my begging, he'd been forced to steal this poison — or, he'd simply gotten tired of living and done it deliberately. The result was the same.

I was orphaned.

The tears took me by surprise. After all, I hadn't loved this man for a long time — or, at least I didn't think I had.

But he'd been my father, and that *mattered.*

I knelt there on the dirt floor beside his body and wept. It kept on until my shoulders shook and my sobs became hoarse and painful. At any moment, I expected him to sit up, cuff me, and tell me to shut up because he was trying to sleep. But, of course, there would be no more cuffs, no more threats, no more yelling.

And yet I grieved.

It took a lot for me to shake myself and get back to what I'd come for. If it had just been for my sake, I'd probably have forgotten the whole thing. But there were Alexandra and Visitor to consider.

So, feeling wrung out and empty, I reached under the cot for what I knew was there, Pop's "Revenge Box."

I slid it out and carried it to the table. It bore no lock, only a latch, one that flipped open so easily that I wondered how many times the old man had done this very thing, if only to gaze down at the vengeance he never took.

Six sticks of dynamite lay inside, along with an equal number of blasting caps. All of it had been carefully wrapped in oil cloth.

How many times had he talked about avenging himself on the town for "throwing me away like trash." I'd always assumed it to be just drunken blather. Then again, he *had* kept these few stolen explosives all this time, hadn't he? So maybe, someday, he might have worked up enough hatred and courage to use them.

I supposed I'd never know.

Quietly, I left that place, taking only the box and an old, cracked lantern that my pop no longer needed.

I never saw that shack or my father again.

By the time I returned to the edge of the brick factory clearing, dawn couldn't have been more than an hour away. That was when Alex and I had guessed Dormer and the menfolk of Van Meter would arrive at the "monster's" lair.

When I reached the tree line, however, I discovered that I'd been wrong.

Dormer and the others were already there.

Watching from a few hundred yards away, I counted at least thirty, all armed for bear. Some had rifles, others shotguns, others revolvers. Among them, their faces lit by the lanterns they carried, I spotted U.G. Griffith, Dr. Alcott, Pete Dunn, O.V. White, and Sid Gregg. Add to that, Mr. Pratt, who strutted around like he owned the place — which, of course, he did — and you had everyone who had ever laid eyes on Visitor. Including me.

Having them there this early — complicated things.

With a nervous sigh, I continued on my way, careful to stay hidden as I circled around the factory grounds and headed toward the creek.

I found Alex — looking like Alex again — and Visitor exactly where we'd agreed, near a small natural crosswalk of steppingstones that spanned the water at one of its widest points. She and I had met here several times over the past months, so often that Alex had once romantically dubbed it, "Our Private Little Bridge."

Visitor was drinking when I stepped from the trees. It was an odd sight, this huge, ungainly creature squatting awkwardly down to reach the water. Standing beside her, Alex gently stroked her flank, speaking not a word but, I suspected, saying a good deal olfactorily.

I almost blurted out, "My pop died," but didn't, and for a couple of reasons. First, Alexandra had enough worries without burdening her with my own, especially when we'd soon be saying good-bye forever. And second, because if I did, I'd likely start keening again—and that was the *last* thing I wanted my dream girl to remember about me.

So, hard as it was—and it was hard—I kept my mouth shut and, recalling the men in the clearing, told her in way of a hello, "We've got a problem."

"I know," she said without facing me. "We smelled them."

"I don't see any way to get back to the mine. We may have to wait them out."

"We can't," Alex replied, turning my way at last. To my alarm, I saw that she'd been crying. "Visitor probably won't survive daylight. I *have* to get her into that mine before the sun fully rises."

We could find a cave, I supposed. But they were all in the direction of the mine, in the direction of the townsmen. I looked at Visitor, who had stopped draining the creek and was now instead nudging her big head toward me, hoping for a petting. The idea of those ignorant, fearful men gunning down this gentle beast sickened me to my core.

"There has to be a way," I said, a little desperately. I looked at Alex, "Can you do the bang-thing again?"

"Bang-thing?"

"When you make them say 'bang' instead of actually firing."

"Oh. Even if I were on the ground, I'm not strong enough to affect more than a few of them at a time. You saw them. How many were there, do you think?"

"Thirty or more," I told her glumly.

As she had before, she came into my arms, pressing her face against my chest. Despite everything, it made my heart swell. It felt good to hold her this way, even in her despair. It felt like I belonged to her, that *we* belonged together.

But, of course, however things worked out in the end, that would never happen.

And my heart, which had just swelled, now broke.

"What if you *weren't* flying?" I asked.

She stopped trembling. "What?"

Gently, and *very* reluctantly, I put my hands on her shoulders and pushed her away from me so I could look into her tear-streaked face. "If you were on the ground with Visitor overhead, could you move among them and keep them 'banging' instead of shooting?"

Her perplexed expression gradually turned into something like hope. "Not all of them all the time. But, if we'd timed it right... maybe..."

"Okay," I said, thinking furiously. Platt had seen two monsters exit the mine, a big one and a small one. For this to work, to *really* work, he would need to see that again. "You can't fly, right?" I asked Alex. "Your wings in the mine were just a trick, a... smell."

"That right."

I said, "Then... could you make *me* look like a little Visitor?"

I could almost hear her gears turning. "I could. But it'd require..." her words trailed off.

"What?" I pressed.

"I... would need to get my scent on you."

"How?" I asked, and I swear before God it felt like the whole world held its breath.

"We would have to... embrace."

"Okay."

"But it would need to be bare skin to bare skin."

"Oh," I heard myself say, more a sigh than a word, I think.

"Awkward," she said with a nervous smile.

"Very." Then I added, "But it's for Visitor."

She nodded. "Yes. For Visitor."

And so, for Visitor's sake, we did it and, for decorum's sake, I won't describe it in any detail. Suffice it to say that it was done there on the edge of the creek, atop a dry cool patch of autumn grass. Now, I had no experience at all in such matters, but I came away certain of two things. First, what Alex and I did during those precious minutes didn't rise to the level of what Pastor Robinson would label "fornication."

But it came close. Very close.

And second, fornication or not, it was still glorious.

Afterward, I was afraid things would be, like Alex had said, awkward. But they weren't. It's hard to explain. We'd done what we did to try to save a creature that Alex loved and that I was learning to love. The fact that we'd both taken joy from the experience was—

—well, it just *was*.

"Hank?"

"Yeah, Al?"

"Are you all right?"

"I'm fine," I said, meaning it, though my face was flushed, and I felt—other things, too. "Are *you* all right?"

She smiled magnificently. "Fine." Then, after a pause, she added, "Thank you."

"You, too," I replied, watching as she dressed, feeling for her soiled frock, which she'd hung over a nearby tree branch. When I started to do the same with my shirt and trousers though, she stopped me. "Don't!"

"Why not?"

"Right now, you've got my scent on you. If you put on your clothes, that'll get mixed with your own. It'll keep it from working."

"You mean I've got to do what's coming... buck naked?"

"I'm afraid so. But they won't see it. They'll just see the illusion of the smaller Visitor."

"Are you sure?"

She nodded. "I'll bring your trousers with me when I meet you at the mine. But that's probably all I can carry and still do what I have to do. Sorry."

I looked down at my skinny, grubby frame, sunken, hairless chest, thin shoulders, and skinny limbs. And, for the first time, I was almost desperately glad that Alex was blind. I didn't want *anybody*, especially not her, to see me in this state.

"It's okay," I said, though it wasn't. "Let's do this thing before I turn chicken."

They were waiting for us.

As Visitor and I cleared the eastern woods, with the first rays of dawn peeking through the trees, I heard shouts of alarm and excitement from the small army of men filling the cleared space between the brick factory and bore hole.

I rode astride Visitor's back, holding on for dear life. I had no Alexandra to cling to this time as the creature beneath me flapped its huge wings and carried us over the field, easily two hundred feet off the ground. A fall from this height would kill me instantly, a fear that wasn't even slightly alleviated when the guns started firing.

I wasn't too worried about the handguns. We were way out of range. But the shotguns concerned me, as did the rifles. I knew most of the men down there. Many were fair shots, but a few were genuine marksmen. Alex had assured me that Visitor's hide could take a bullet or two. But mine couldn't. So, if Alex didn't manage her part in this mad scheme, I'd likely be dead in moments.

Then I heard, "Bang!"

And again, "Bang!"

Then a voice called, "What the Sam Hill are you guys doing?"

"Bang! Bang! Bang!"

That's when I spotted her, a delicate figure moving amongst the men, none of whom seemed to pay her the slightest attention. But everywhere she went, the men closest to her stopped firing and instead uttered that same nonsense word, much to the confusion and annoyance of those around them.

Alex had my pants over her shoulder, carried the box of dynamite in the crook of one slender arm, and held my father's old lantern in her opposite hand. Despite that, this supposedly blind girl moved like a deer among the armed men and somehow remained unseen. Alex Harrer was stronger than me, smarter than me, and from somewhere completely beyond my understanding.

I was in love with an alien.

"Bang! Bang! Bang!"

Visitor banked left; her movements smooth. Even so, I cried out as I felt myself start to slide off her back. Then to my surprise, her hindquarters gave a little jerk, which was enough to nudge me once more into the right position.

My ride, it seemed, was looking out for me.

"Good girl," I whispered.

She offered me a bleat in reply.

"Shoot! Damn you all, shoot!" That was Dormer; I felt sure of it. The deputy was almost directly beneath us, his revolver aimed skyward and firing over and over with each passing second. Like I said, I hadn't been too worried about the handguns, but Dormer was better with his than most and I actually felt two bullets whiz past me on their way to the moon.

This time, I cried out in alarm.

So did Visitor, her whole body jerking so hard that I worried she'd been hit.

Then, without warning, Dormer yelled, "Bang! Bang!" This drew befuddled glances from the men flanking him, though not one of them noticed the slip of a blonde girl as she hurried through their ranks.

That was how it went. Visitor and I—looking, Alex had assured me, as if the previously spotted "little monster" were flying alongside the "big monster"—crossed the open ground between the tree line and the mine entrance in less than a minute. Meanwhile, Alex moved beneath us. She couldn't turn *all* the bullets into harmless "bangs," or even most of them. But she could, and did, make certain that the townsmen directly beneath us, the ones with the shortest range and the clearest shots, never pulled their triggers.

Without warning, Visitor went into a dive.

I yelped and threw myself across her broad back, wrapping my arms as far over her shoulders as they'd reach. Suddenly, the ground, with the black bore hole like a bullseye in its center, rose up to meet us much faster than I would have liked.

"It's getting away!" someone lamented.

"Keep shooting, all of you!" Dormer commanded. "Bang! Bang! Bang!"

An instant later, darkness swallowed us up.

Visitor, perhaps caught up in the victorious spirit of the moment, or maybe just desperately relieved like me, uttered a single loud, long bleat. Then, as she touched down at the bottom of the main shaft, engulfed in darkness, I slid off of her and let my feet rejoice at having solid ground beneath them once more.

With a nervous laugh, I stroked Visitor's flank. In response, she turned her huge head and nuzzled my armpit. "Tell you what, girl," I said, still laughing. "Let's not do that again, okay?"

She uttered an oddly dog-like chuff, as if in agreement.

Then I heard a sound behind me and, as I spun around, Alex all but jumped into my arms.

She'd come down the steps a lot faster than I'd gone up them.

I won't describe how it felt to hold her again, especially given that I was still naked as a newborn. All I will say is that it both pleased me and hurt my already breaking heart. She felt so alive, so real, so utterly—human.

"You did it, Hank!" she exclaimed, squeezing me tightly. Too tightly.

Nope, I thought. *This won't do.*

It took some effort, but I managed to pull myself away from her. Then, realizing my predicament, she wordlessly handed me my trousers. The shirt and shoes were still back at the creek, but this was a far sight better than nothing. Quickly and gratefully, I pulled them on.

Just in time, too, because sounds came from above us, at the lip of the borehole. I couldn't make out the words, but the tone seemed clear enough. The townsmen, still led by Dormer, were trying to decide whether or not to risk following us into the mine.

"We have to go," Alex told me, and I took slight comfort from the sorrow in her voice.

"Then let's go," I said, using one of my two remaining matches to light Pop's old lantern.

With both Visitor's horn light and Pop's old lantern leading the way, we found the collapsed shaft easily enough.—though, looking into it now, I wasn't at all sure we had enough dynamite to do the job. "We might be just as likely to bring the ceiling down on our heads as to unplug that hole," I said to Alex as she placed the box on the floor and explored its contents with deft fingers.

"That depends on how smart we are with the placement," she assured me, and something in her tone made me think she knew more about this sort of business than I'd imagined. Then again, might not a race of folks living deep underground understand a thing or two about demolition? "Don't worry, once I'm down there, I can put them where they need to go."

"I only got one match left," I said.

"One is all I'll need. Give it here."

"You sure?" I asked, handing it over. "I mean… Alex, you can't see."

"Hank Trotter," she admonished, though not unkindly. "I would think you'd know better than that by now."

And, of course, I did. But knowing and accepting, it turns out, aren't always the same thing. "Sorry," I muttered.

She cupped my face in her hands, and for one breathtaking moment, I thought she meant to kiss me. Instead, she said, "Don't say that. You have nothing to be sorry for. I'm the one who's sorry. I should have trusted you. I should have told you everything, especially when Visitor came looking for me. I didn't think you'd be able to deal with it. But here you are, doing just that. Visitor and I owe you a debt we can never repay." She stepped back from me, which let me at least catch my breath. "Now take her up the tunnel aways. I don't want either of you nearby when this dynamite goes off."

"What about you?" I asked.

"I'll be right as rain." And the way she said it made me believe her.

So, I put a hand on Visitor's shoulder. "Come on, girl." To my surprise, she came without protest, though she did look nervously back at her mistress before following me away from the shaft and out of sight.

I didn't know how long it would take. I didn't know exactly how the blasting caps worked. Maybe I should have —

A deafening explosion shook the floor and walls of the tunnel, setting dust and small chunks of rock raining down on the two of us. Visitor crowed and ducked her head under my arm. At the same time, and quite remarkably, she opened one wing and used it to shield *me*, rather like a big umbrella. It was a sweet, generous gesture from a creature who'd received the poorest of welcomes from the human race, and I was gripped by a sharp, stinging sense of shame for my species.

We should have been better than that.

"Sorry, girl," I muttered.

Only a few moments passed, but they were *long* moments. Finally, I called down the tunnel, "Al! You okay?"

There was no reply.

Visitor crowed again.

"Alex Harrer! After all this, you better not be dead!" I made a joke of it, though a sick knot had settled in the pit of my stomach.

"I'm okay!" came her reply, though it was wrapped in a hoarse dry cough. "Just waiting for the debris to settle."

Well, Visitor and I were done waiting. Together, and with no coaxing at all, we went back up the tunnel. Yes, there was dust here, a lot of it, forcing me to cover my mouth and nose with one hand. But the ceiling and walls seemed to be intact. Even better, Alex stood beside the shaft, peering down into it with a nose that twitched, almost like a rabbit's.

"Did that do it?" I asked, though talking made me cough.

She nodded as, around us, the dust cleared. Her delicate features were caked over with dirt, her blonde hair almost black from it. But she was smiling. "The way's clear," she finally said.

As I looked at my dream girl, Visitor nuzzled her way under my arm again.

Finally, I asked, "Can I come with you?"

Her mouth worked. Fresh tears suddenly spilled down her cheeks, clearing paths in the grime. "You can't survive down there, Hank. The air's... not the same. And it's too hot for you."

"Then can you take her home?" I asked, trying not to sound as desperate as I felt. "And then come back?"

She cried harder. "I don't think they'll let me. I told you. No one's ever stayed on the surface so long. I'm probably going to be in a lot of trouble."

"I ain't never going to see you again?"

She shook her head.

I straightened my spine. "Then I want to *see* you."

"What?"

"I want to see what you really look like."

"No," she said at once.

"Please, Al."

"No! You won't… you won't want to look at me!" Her tears turned into sobs.

But I wasn't giving up, not this time. "Alexandra Harrer, after that pretty speech you made before, you still don't trust me?"

"I…" Her words trailed off. Then she seemed to steady herself and replied, "Alright."

She spared a moment to bend over and shake some of the debris out of her hair. Then, as she rubbed at her forehead and both her cheeks, it suddenly struck me: *She's making herself as presentable as she can.*

The realization did a lot of things to my already rent heart.

An instant later, Alex *changed.*

It wasn't a transformation, exactly, but more like a "sluffing off." The mechanism behind it was a mystery to me—but I guessed it involved more olfactory manipulation, though I didn't smell anything different.

In Alex's place, however, there was now a long-limbed, fine-boned glowing creature wearing her soiled frock. The blonde hair was gone, replaced with a smooth scalp and remarkably big ears. The nose was flat and broad, the nostrils large. They opened and closed continually, no doubt drawing information from the air. The mouth was a thin line, not quite lipless.

And there were no eyes, none at all.

I stared at her, my breath catching. She stood before me, her arms at her sides, as if waiting for something. It was then that I noticed tears. They still fell, though now they came from small slits beside her nose.

Her mouth opened and words came out. She didn't speak them exactly, forming them as I would with tongue and lip. Instead, they just sort of came forth from the small, delicate, pink maw. "This is me, Hank."

My voice caught, but I worked through it. "You're beautiful."

"I'm not like you," she said. "I'm not human."

"You're the most human person I've ever known," I told her, meaning every word. Then, leaving Visitor behind me, I marched forward, cupped her face as she had mine, and kissed those small glowing lips. It was the first time I'd ever been bold enough to attempt such a thing, and half of me expected her to recoil in alarm or even disgust. But she didn't.

She just kissed me back.

I held her for most of a minute, until Visitor bleated, and I thought maybe I could hear distant voices in the mine.

"We... have to go," Alex said as we parted.

"I love you."

"What?"

"I've loved you since the moment we met."

"Hank... I..."

"You don't have to say it back. Frankly, I think it'll break what little's left of my heart if you do. Just take her and go. Be safe. And live a good life down there."

Alexandra's alien body shuddered, and I realized she was sobbing again. She took my hand in both of hers and kissed it. After that, she motioned to Visitor, who hurried forward to stand at her side.

Then my dream girl treated me to one last smile. It was a small thing. I wasn't sure if her people even had teeth. But it was real and full of gratitude — and affection, if nothing else.

I smiled back.

And, just like that, the two of them jumped into the shaft and out of my life.

I stood there for a long time. To this day, I don't know how long. I felt utterly empty, drained of all feeling. There was no pain, no fear. But neither was there hope or joy. Hope and joy had just left me forever.

Finally, because I could think of nothing better to do, I abandoned the shaft and headed back toward the surface, using Pop's old broken lantern to guide my steps.

And that was where they found me.

And arrested me.

<h1 style="text-align:center">Chapter Seven</h1>

Back in the cell.

Gone was Dormer's deference to me; I didn't even get a shirt or shoes to wear. Gone were the sympathetic looks from even the kindest townsfolk, like Peter and Sid Gregg. They, along with many others as the day wore on, visited the deputy's office on various pretexts, only to ogle or glare at the beggar-boy who was somehow in league with the monster that had "terrorized" their town for a week.

At one point in the afternoon, Moira Van Meter swept in, screamed at both Dormer and me, and insisted that I be hanged from the nearest tree for "taking away my sweet Alexandra." No one had gone so far as to accuse me of actually killing the girl, not yet anyway. But I knew it was coming. The townsfolk wanted a scapegoat, and it seemed they liked the look of my horns.

As for myself, I was consumed by a kind of emptiness. My father was dead. I'd told Dormer about finding him in the shack and the deputy had promised to have him looked after. But I knew what that meant: a pauper's grave with a simple wooden cross for a marker. Nobody had cared about him, just like nobody cared about me. My only friend was gone forever, leaving me alone in world of familiar strangers—and, from Dormer's general demeanor, I had the grim feeling that Moira would, in the end, get what she wanted.

Before too long, I'd end up in the ground beside Pop.

And maybe that was just fine.

After all, what promise did life hold for me now?

As for the creature that had caused so much fear, no one seemed inclined to talk about it, at least not when Dormer or me were in earshot. The handful of men brave enough to descend into the abandoned mine didn't go far, held back first by Visitor's loud crowing and then by the sound of an explosion deep in the tunnels. What I'd heard of them while saying my good-byes to Alex had been echoes from hundreds of feet above us. Sound travels strangely underground. She'd had been right about that.

I didn't say much to anyone. Dormer tried questioning me but gave up when I didn't respond. He warned me that the sheriff would be coming by morning, and that I'd likely be moved to Des Moines for "further investigation," and that "being silent wasn't going to help me once that happened."

It was probably true—but that didn't make me care.

Finally, as the day's shadows grew long, Dormer brought me a simple dinner, sort of grunted when I thanked him, and then went to work behind his desk. To be fair, the man looked exhausted, a condition worsened by the fact that he didn't dare leave me alone here, not when I'd somehow escaped from custody two nights before. So, as the sun set, there he stayed, my guard and minder, leaving me to lie on the cot and stare dismally at the ceiling as the long hours ticked by.

I didn't know what time it was when it happened, but I could have made an educated guess.

1 a.m.

I hadn't been able to sleep, despite being as exhausted as the deputy. Too much had occurred. Too much had been taken from me. The idea of closing my eyes, only to wake and remember everything I'd lost was simply more than I could bear.

"Hank?"

I sat bolt upright on the cot. The cell was in shadow, though a lamp still glowed at the corner of Dormer's desk. By its light, I could see the deputy. He was sitting up in his chair, his back straight and his eyes open. One hand held a pencil, though neither the hand nor pencil seemed to be moving. In fact, Lucas Dormer appeared more statue than man, motionless and staring at nothing.

I scrambled to my feet and peered through the bars. What I saw almost knocked me back down. It sounds melodramatic, I know. But it's true.

Alexandra Harrer stood in front of the open door.

Various possibilities flashed through my mind, each one on the tail of the last. I was dreaming. I was dead. Grief had torn away my sanity. But I swear, I never once considered that what I saw might be real, not until she stepped up to the bars, reached in, and touched my face.

"Alex?" I whispered.

"It's me, Hank."

"You… you didn't make it home?"

She smiled. She was wearing a flowered summer dress, though where she'd gotten it was hardly a concern right now. She was also clean, her hair washed and her skin as glowingly porcelain as ever. "I did," she said. "And, as it turned out, I wasn't in as much trouble as I thought."

"You've… come… back?" I asked, the words almost painful. But this was no time to get mealy mouthed, so I added, "For *me*?"

"For you," she replied. "Mostly."

"Mostly?"

"Let's get you out of there."

"But Deputy Dormer!" I protested. "He—"

"He's… paused."

"Paused?"

"He'll be fine. Here, I have the key."

She opened the cell door, and I immediately pulled her to me—largely, I admit, to prove to myself that she wasn't a figment of my imagination. We held each other for more than a minute. She smelled like strawberries, her skin warm and alive and unmistakably real.

Finally, she said, "Come on." Then she led me by the hand through the office and outside.

The night was surprisingly bright, making me suspect a harvest moon. But before I could confirm that suspicion, I noticed that the street was far from empty. Despite the hour, no less than a dozen people milled about, probably in readiness for another "attack" by the "monster."

The crazy thing, however, was that the "monster" was already *here*.

Visitor stood in the middle of Main Street, bleating a welcome as she regarded me. And the people—I counted eight men and four women—took no notice of her at all. In fact, none of them were moving, not a muscle, as much statues as Dormer had become.

"What's going on?" I asked, laughing as Visitor hopped up to me and shoved her big head under my arm.

"Well, I couldn't very well leave you to take the blame for everything, now could I?" Alex replied. "Besides, Visitor's taken a shine to you. She was inconsolable after we left."

"Just Visitor?"

Alex blushed. "Maybe not just her."

"What have you done to everybody?"

"Nothing," she assured me. "They're fine. Like I told you, they're just paused."

"Why?"

"Well, partly to keep poor Visitor from getting shot at again, and partly so that their memories can be… adjusted."

"Adjusted?" I asked.

"Once we're gone, they'll resume their lives just fine," Alex explained. "But they won't remember me… or you. They *will* remember Visitor, however. She's too… well, 'big' a memory to completely remove. But their collective narrative will be somewhat… abbreviated."

I chuckled. "That's a lot of big words, Al. I'm just a poor country boy."

"You need a broad vocabulary if you want to be a writer."

"So, you did this to get me out, wipe all memory of me, and… what? Let me leave town?"

She nodded. "Start over somewhere new."

My humor evaporated like smoke. "I don't think I can do that. I don't think I know how to be that alone."

"Who said anything about you being alone?" Alex asked. Then she cradled my face and kissed me—hard. It was the best kiss I'd ever had, ever imagined having, and I felt it all the way to my toes. My arms closed around her, and it was all I could do not to cry into her open mouth. Sensing this, she slowly broke the kiss and drew my head down to her shoulder. "How's your heart, Hank?"

"My heart?"

"Better than it was down in the mine?"

"Yeah," I replied, choking back a sob. "Definitely, yeah."

"Then you should know that I love you, too. And I have since the day we met."

That set me off even more. But she was patient and held me without comment or complaint. Finally, my emotions spent, I straightened and self-consciously wiped at my eyes. Visitor nuzzled me again, rubbing her head against my back. I laughed and hugged her around the neck, which she clearly liked.

"Where will we go?" I asked Alex.

"We'll figure that out together, all three of us."

"Three?" I asked.

She nodded to Visitor. "You don't think I'm going to leave her again, did you?"

Already, my thoughts were churning. We'd need to go somewhere remote, somewhere with lots of open space where a strange, winged creature could fly through the night without anyone seeing her. We'd also need a safe place for her to stay during the daylight hours. And we'd need a home for ourselves and our—

"Alex?"

"Yes, Hank?"

"Can we... have kids?"

The question seemed to surprise her. For a minute, she simply stood there, her blind eyes not quite regarding me. Then she shrugged and said, "I don't know. But I'm kind of keen to find out."

That made me kiss her again.

"Last question," I told her when we parted once more. "How did you do all this? I mean... the whole town? I didn't think you had that kind of power!"

"I don't," she told me, smiling broadly. Then she stepped back and raised one finger skyward. "But *they* do."

And, for the first time since she'd led me out of the deputy's office, I looked up.

There was no harvest moon.

Instead, the sky was *filled* with Visitors. There had to be a hundred of them, maybe more, all with their wings spread, beating at the air in such a way as to keep them in place. And, on their backs, riding them as I had over the mine, were the same number of Alex's people. They glowed like angels, all of them looking down on us and smiling those little alien smiles.

"I have a big family," Alex revealed just before kissing me a third time, the third of many.

Hope and joy, it seemed, had found me after all.

About the Author

Ty Drago is a full-time writer and the author of ten published novels, including his five-book *Undertakers* series (optioned for a feature film), *Dragons*, an SF genre-bender, and *Rags*, an edgy YA horror novel set in Atlantic City. He's also the founder, publisher, and managing editor of ALLEGORY (www.allegoryezine.com), a highly successful online magazine that, for more than twenty years, has featured speculative fiction by new and established authors worldwide.

Ty's horror novel, *St. Damned*, will be released in 2025, as will his historical saga, *The New Americans*. He's just completed *Angelfire*, a modern retelling of the Orpheus legend.

He lives in New Jersey with his ever-patient wife Helene, one needy dog, and three goofy hens.

artist's rendition of the Van Meter Visitor

VAN METER VISITOR

ORIGINS: A regional cryptid, the Van Meter Visitor hails from the state of Iowa. First sighted in Van Meter in 1903, there have been reports of other encounters in the state as recently as 2020.

DESCRIPTION: Depending on the account, the Van Meter Visitor has been described as a winged bipedal half-human, half-animal creature standing as much as nine feet tall, or presenting as five feet long in flight. The wings are described as bat-like, but the creature is also said to resemble a modern spoonbill or a pterodactyle. By some accounts, the wings were large enough to obscure the sky when flapping.

Other than its grand stature, this cryptid is said to have a horn protruding from its forehead that emits a beam of light, and it emanates a powerful stench said to disrupt the thoughts and memory of those nearby.

A plaster cast was made of a three-toed clawed depression believed to be its footprint.

Some witnesses claimed that it hopped like a kangaroo, but others said it moved with great speed across the rooftops.

Though multiple people reported firing guns at the creature, they claim it was to no effect.

LIFE CYCLE: While there are no specific details about the creature's reproduction, there have been sightings of multiple Visitors of varying sizes, making plausible the consideration that a population exists, whether the variance in size denotes young or gendered individuals, there is insufficient data to determine.

HISTORY: The original encounter is documented to have taken place in Van Meter, Iowa in September and October of 1903. Over the course of five nights, multiple well-respected individuals reportedly engaged with the Van Meter Visitor.

When the sightings continued the residents of the town formed a posse and tracked the creatures to a nearby abandoned mine. At the first the creatures flew off; when they returned, they descended into the mine, ignoring those firing upon them.

Though the townfolk left no further documentation of

encounters, there have been other reports.

One such encounter took place near the abandoned mine in the 1980, where new residents out for a walk reported a massive bird-like creature flying overhead.

In 2000, a family driving home to Van Meter reported seeing a corpse of a Visitor on the side of the road, but when the father went back to look it was gone.

Other such occurrences have been reported in the nearby area as recently as 2020.

While there are theories as to the true nature of the Van Meter Visitor, including but not limited to the possibility of misidentification, it being an undiscovered species, and the belief that it is a trans-dimensional being, any true determination cannot be reached without further evidence.

About the Artist

Until his decades-long disappearance, JW Harp was known for his trippy underground comic strip *Captain Thetan*, about a seafarer who controls reality for himself and others. This otherworldly character appeared in a dozen issues of the classic rare underground zine *Sandanista Romp*. JW has reemerged thanks largely to eSpec Books' Systema Paradoxa series. In 2023, JW started Skilletfire Studios with comic-book author Scott Eckelaert. Under the Skilletfire Studios mantle, JW has produced the graphic novel *Boylon Heights*, and the *Gimme Five Comics* series. Since its launch, *Gimme Five Comics* has included work by Artyom Topilin, Elena Cerisciola, John L. French, Keith Lansdale, and Joe R. Lansdale with more to come.

JW grew up in the seedy parts of South Carolina, which is all of it. He feels part Canadian and part Costa Rican these days. He lives in North Carolina. Please get in touch with him at jwharp@skilletfire.com.

Capture the Cryptids!

Cryptid Crate is a monthly subscription box filled with various cryptozoology and paranormal-themed items to wear, display, and collect. Expect a carefully curated box filled with creeptastic pieces from indie makers and artisans pertaining to bigfoot, sasquatch, UFOs, ghosts, and other cryptid and mysterious creatures (apparel, decor, media, etc).

Now Featuring Cryptid Crate Jr!

http://CryptidCrate.com

www.ingramcontent.com/pod-product-compliance
Lightning Source LLC
Chambersburg PA
CBHW031753200726
48289CB00013B/907